PRAISE FOR TH~~E~~ QUINN S~~ERIES~~

"Brilliant and heart pounding"

JEFFERY DEAVER, *NEW YORK TIMES*
BESTSELLING AUTHOR

"Addictive."

JAMES ROLLINS, *NEW YORK TIMES*
BESTSELLING AUTHOR

"Unputdownable."

TESS GERRITSEN, *NEW YORK TIMES*
BESTSELLING AUTHOR

"The best elements of Lee Child, John le Carré, and Robert Ludlum."

SHELDON SIEGEL, *NEW YORK TIMES*
BESTSELLING AUTHOR

"Quinn is one part James Bond, one part Jason Bourne."

NASHVILLE BOOK WORM

"Welcome addition to the political thriller game."

PUBLISHERS WEEKLY

THE DAMAGED

ALSO BY BRETT BATTLES

Takedown

STANDALONES

Novels

The Pull of Gravity

No Return

Mine

Novellas

Mine: The Arrival

Short Stories

"Perfect Gentleman"

For Younger Readers

THE TROUBLE FAMILY CHRONICLES

Here Comes Mr. Trouble

THE DAMAGED

A JONATHAN QUINN NOVEL

BRETT BATTLES

1

FIFTEEN YEARS AGO · HONOLULU, HAWAII

"He's getting out of his car," Peyton whispered over the comm. He was stationed in front of the Royal Hawaiian Hotel, playing the part of a tourist waiting for his family to join him. "Same two bodyguards as before. They're approaching the door now."

"Kells?" Jacko said from inside the hotel suite cabinet where he was hiding, seven floors up.

"In position," Kells said. She was sitting in a chair in the hotel's lobby.

"See them?" Peyton asked.

A few seconds later, Kells said, "Got 'em. They're passing reception.... Hold on. Stopping."

The radio fell silent.

"What's happening?" Jacko asked.

"They're talking," Kells replied.

"Can you hear them?"

"No. Not close enough.... Okay, one of the bodyguards is walking over to the reception desk. The other one and the target are heading to the elevators. What do you want me to do?"

Jacko said, "Elevator."

"Copy."

"Peyton, reposition to the lobby and keep an eye on the bodyguard."

"Copy."

Jacko could hear movement over the comm, then from Kells, a nearly inaudible "Almost there."

Fifteen seconds of silence were followed by a ding and the sound of elevator doors sliding open. Movement again.

"Floor?" a low male voice asked.

"Nine, please," Kells said. "Thank you."

Jacko heard the elevator doors close again, followed by the car beginning its ascent.

"On holiday or business?" another male voice asked, this one not as deep, with a slight, eastern European accent. Jacko recognized it as belonging to Jan Masiar, the target.

"Holiday," Kells said. "Just arrived this morning."

"Is that right? From where?"

"Seattle."

"Beautiful city. Traveling with family?" Masiar asked.

"Three girlfriends, actually," she said, acting like someone who never gave a second thought to personal safety.

"Well, that sounds like fun."

The bell dinged again.

"I hope you enjoy your stay," Masiar said. "Perhaps we will see each other again."

Kells said nothing, but Jacko had no doubt she gave Masiar an encouraging smile.

The sound of the doors opening, then movement, and the doors closing again.

"He's on seven," Kells said.

"Nice job. I think he'd have taken you with him if you'd suggested it."

"Gross."

"Peyton, update on the other bodyguard?"

"Still at the front desk," Peyton said. "He's talking to a

manager. I did a walk-by and it sounded like they were discussing the use of one of the meeting rooms."

"Copy."

Jan Masiar owned several manufacturing plants in Slovakia and was in Honolulu for an industry convention. It was only natural he would need space for a meeting.

Manufacturing wasn't his only business, however. As a former general in the Slovakian army, with strong ties to many still in power, he had developed a very lucrative side business selling NATO secrets to Russia. For the most part he played it smart by passing on low-level intel he undoubtedly thought couldn't be traced back to him. Initially that was true.

But success bred overconfidence, which had a funny way of breeding mistakes. And one piece of intelligence turned out to have great significance. Its delivery to the Russians resulted in the capture and execution of three valuable NATO informants in Moscow. A covert but intense investigation had been launched to find out how this had happened. In only a matter of weeks, it'd led to the former general, and to the realization that his traitorous behavior had been going on for a while. A termination order was given, and Jacko and his team had been sent to carry it out.

From beyond the cabinet, Jacko heard the suite's door open. He turned on his palm-sized monitor. It was wirelessly connected to a camera he had hidden on the wall by the windows. The lens provided a view of the front door and most of the main room.

He watched as the bodyguard entered, a gun now in his hand, while Masiar stayed in the public corridor. The guard made his way through the room, checking behind furniture and curtains. When he started to open cabinets, Jacko couldn't help but tense a little. The doors he was hiding behind were the fourth set the man opened, but as Jacko knew would be the case, the man did not see him.

That morning, Masiar had received a "gift" of two dozen high-end bottles of whiskey and tequila and rum, from the vice president of a company he had met at the conference who wanted to do business with him. The VP had been Jacko, and Peyton had been the hotel bellhop who had brought up the liquor.

When Peyton had suggested stashing the lot in the cabinets near the bar, Masiar had agreed. Each bottle was packaged inside a box, and they formed a perfect wall behind which Jacko could hide. If Masiar had said no to the cabinets or refused the delivery altogether, the team would have had to go with a less desirable option, which was a nonissue now.

The bodyguard went into the bedroom, where he stayed for nearly two minutes. When he reappeared, he walked calmly toward the main door, his gun back in his shoulder holster.

"All clear," he said and exited the suite.

Masiar entered and shut the door. Alone now, at least in his mind, he tossed his suit jacket on the couch and walked over to the bar, only a meter from the cabinet where Jacko was. Masiar poured himself a whiskey neat, from one of the three bottles Peyton had conveniently left on the counter.

He walked over and sat on the couch, drink in hand. After taking a sip, he turned on the TV and flipped through channels, finally settling on CNN.

"Bodyguard's on the move again," Peyton reported from the lobby. "Looks like he's heading upstairs."

Jacko clicked his mic once in acknowledgment.

Three minutes later, there was a knock at the door.

Not moving from his seat, Masiar yelled, "What?"

A muffled response came from beyond the door. Jacko assumed it was a report on the discussion with the hotel manager, but the bodyguard's voice was incomprehensible.

"All right," Masiar said. "That will be fine. One hour, then."

Another answer, shorter this time.

Masiar said nothing after the bodyguard finished speaking. He sipped his whiskey and watched TV until the drink was finished. He then headed into the bedroom, unbuttoning his shirt on the way.

Jacko clicked his microphone twice, paused, then twice again, signaling it was showtime.

He moved the boxes out of his way, opened the cabinet door, and quietly crawled out. From the bedroom doorway, he could hear water running from a faucet in the master bathroom. He peeked around the jamb and saw Masiar's shirt lying across the end of the bed.

The water stopped.

Jacko pulled back into the main room and pressed himself against the wall, in case the target reentered the bedroom. But then the shower came on.

He smiled. This was the moment he'd been waiting for.

He slipped into the bedroom and shut the door, to reduce the chances of any unusual sounds reaching the guards outside the suite. He pulled a pillbox out of his pocket and removed the capsule. With his gun in one gloved hand and the capsule in the other, he approached the bathroom. From the splats of water hitting the floor, he knew Masiar was indeed in the shower.

Jacko had reconned the bathroom when he first arrived. It was a large space, with a standalone tub at the far end and a long counter with dual sinks to the left of the doorway. A privacy wall protruded from the entrance on the right side, preventing anyone from seeing directly into the shower.

Jacko moved along this wall and peered around the end at the double-wide glass shower.

Masiar stood in the middle of the stream, face tilted up, eyes closed. Every few seconds he ran his hands over his head, squeegeeing water onto his back. Next came a round of lathering, followed by another rinse. After another minute of just standing under the showerhead, Masiar turned off the water.

As soon as the target opened the door, Jacko swung around the wall, his gun pointed at Masiar's face. "Not a sound. Nod if you understand."

Masiar froze, his eyes wide.

"*Nod* if you understand," Jacko repeated.

Masiar nodded.

"Good. Now turn around."

"What do you want?"

Usually Jacko wouldn't have hesitated to smack a guy with the barrel of his gun for not following directions, but one of the conditions of the mission was to avoid any obvious body marks. So, he chose instead to stick the gun in the man's face. "Do it."

As soon as Masiar turned, Jacko smashed the capsule against the base of the man's neck, directly over his spinal cord. The shell broke and the gel-like liquid inside flowed onto the man's skin, where it would be quickly absorbed.

Masiar jerked and tried to reach around for the spot.

Jacko slapped the man's hand away. "Don't."

Apparently, not all of the old soldier had left Masiar. He whirled around and grabbed for Jacko's gun. Jacko yanked the pistol back and shoved the older man in the chest with his free hand.

Masiar stumbled backward into the shower and slipped on the wet tiles. His legs flew out from under him and down he went, whacking his head against the back wall and landing with a thud.

Jacko tensed, ready for the son of a bitch to jump back up, but Masiar remained on the floor, unmoving. Jacko kicked the man's foot, thinking he might be faking, but the target's leg moved without resistance.

Jacko took a step into the shower and saw blood pooling under Masiar's head, some of it flowing toward the drain.

He checked the man's pulse.

There was none.

"Well, shit."

The target had gone and killed himself a full minute before the drug would have done the job. And in a messier fashion, too.

He stared at the body.

The gel would have terminated Masiar without leaving a trace, and after the cleaner set the scene, even the bodyguards would have been fooled into believing the target had died of natural causes.

But maybe the way things had worked out wasn't so bad. People died in showers all the time, didn't they?

Yeah. Yeah, they did.

This would work. Bonus: the cleaner wouldn't have that much to do now.

Speaking of.

Jacko clicked on his mic. "Jacko for Durrie."

"Go for Durrie," the cleaner replied.

"Target down. I'm ready for you."

2

Durrie looked over at Angel Ortega. "Hit it."

Ortega turned on the electric motor and lowered the window-washer scaffold two stories to the seventh floor, outside the suite Masiar was renting. Specifically, to the windows of the suite's bedroom.

Durrie and Ortega raised the screen they'd rigged to the side of the scaffold opposite the building, concealing what they were about to do from the view of anyone on the ground or in the surrounding structures.

"In position," Durrie said as soon as the blind was up. "You ready?"

Inside, the curtain pulled back, revealing Jacko, the ops leader.

After a nod from Durrie, Ortega attached two suction-cupped glass handles to the pane, then placed a premeasured, ten-layer strip of cloth over the windowsill, anchoring it with painter's tape. From a spray bottle with a straw-directed outlet, he applied a heat-activated solvent to the rubber holding the glass in place, all the way around the pane.

No matter how much of the work Durrie made Ortega do, the kid never complained. Which was great, given that Durrie was sick of doing the crap work. He preferred to focus his efforts on more interesting things.

When Ortega had finished with the spray, he picked up the acetylene torch. "Live fire," he warned, and lit the device.

"I got this," Durrie said, reaching for the torch. This was more interesting. And besides, with Jacko watching on the other side of the window, he needed to do something.

While Durrie ran the flame over the treated rubber, Ortega held on to the suction handles. The solution was fast acting, and as soon as the torch passed over a spot, the rubber underneath instantly turned to liquid that ran down the glass to the waiting cloth.

After the circuit was complete and the rubber was no longer doing its job, the glass rocked back and forth in the frame. It could not, however, be pulled out just yet.

Durrie took over holding the glass, while Ortega used an electric screwdriver with a specially designed bit to unscrew the metal frame. As each piece came free, he set it on the scaffolding.

The trickiest part of the operation came after the last piece of metal was removed. Working together, Durrie and Ortega very carefully pulled the pane away from the building and set it on the scaffolding.

A quick inspection of the glass revealed no cracks or nicks, just streaks where the melted rubber had run down. Ortega would deal with that.

"You good?" Durrie asked.

"Yes, sir," Ortega replied.

That was another thing Durrie liked about Ortega. Respect. That was how a number two should always act.

Durrie picked up his duffel and stepped through the open window into Masiar's suite. He glanced around but the only other person in the room was Jacko. "Where's the body?"

"There's been a slight...adjustment to the plan," Jacko said.

"What the hell does that mean?"

Jacko led him into the bathroom.

There was the body, naked and sprawled in the shower, blood surrounding the man's head and much of his upper torso.

"*Slight* adjustment?" Durrie said. "What happened to dying in his sleep?"

"He slipped right after I applied the drug."

Durrie looked at Jacko, an eyebrow raised. "Slipped."

"I can't help it if he was clumsy."

Durrie turned back to the body. "Was he at least alive long enough to absorb the drug?"

"I don't think so. I wiped the back of his neck just in case." He grabbed a plastic bag off the counter. Inside was one of the hotel's hand towels. "You'll want to get rid of this."

Durrie grunted and took the bag from him. "You applied it to the base of the neck?"

"Yeah."

"Nowhere else?"

"Nowhere else."

Durrie would give the body an extra wipe-down himself, to make sure all exterior traces of the drug were gone. The last thing they needed was for some civilian to accidently get some of it on his or her skin and die. Not that Durrie actually cared about a random civilian, but he knew a complication like that would blow back on him, even though he wasn't the one who screwed things up.

"So, I take it we're just going to leave him like this," he said.

Jacko shrugged. "It's as good as dying in bed."

"Awesome," Durrie replied without conviction.

A cleaner was someone you called when you needed a body removed or staged. Sure, some actual cleaning was usually involved, but that was always in service of the large mission. This job was shaping up to be *only* cleaning.

And that was bullshit.

Unfortunately, it was bullshit Durrie couldn't do anything about.

He sighed. "Tell me where you've been."

Jacko showed him and Durrie got to work.

With Masiar's bodyguards standing outside the suite's entrance, vacuuming for stray hairs and skin cells was out of the question. So Durrie stuck to cleaning all surfaces Jacko might have touched, starting with a full wipe-down of the inside of the cabinet the ops leader had been hiding in. Durrie then returned to the bedroom to deal with everything there, closing the door behind him.

It was the kind of work any newbie, no matter his specialty, could have done. Durrie considered switching places with Ortega, but then Durrie would have been stuck on the scaffold, making sure the glass didn't plummet to the ground. That was not his idea of a fun afternoon.

None of this was his idea of a fun afternoon.

Despite all his complaining, it took him only seven minutes to complete everything, including a second pass on the back of Masiar's neck. Durrie handed his trash out to Ortega, and, more out of habit than a desire to be thorough, made a final sweep of the bedroom and bathroom. As he was walking back to the window, he heard a noise from beyond the closed door to the other room, followed by someone saying, "Mr. Masiar?"

Durrie sprinted to the window.

At the desk across the room, Jacko was in the middle of cloning the information off of Masiar's laptop onto a portable drive. He looked over, surprised at Durrie's sudden movement. Before Jacko could question it, the voice in the other room spoke again, much closer this time.

"Mr. Masiar?"

Out of the corner of his eye, Durrie saw Jacko jump up from the desk chair, but he couldn't have cared less about the assassin. His focus was on saving his own ass. He slipped through the window, pulled the curtain closed behind him, and said to Ortega, "The glass, now!"

"What about—"

"The glass!"

Ortega grabbed the glass and started putting it back into place. As he set the bottom edge into its groove, Jacko ducked around the curtain, then jammed his hands against the inside frame to keep his momentum from sending him straight into the glass.

"What the hell?" he whispered. "Move it."

Ortega pulled the glass back and Jacko climbed onto the scaffold. As soon as he was out of the way, Ortega reseated the glass, getting the final edge in place at the same moment they heard the bedroom door open.

"Hold it still," Jacko whispered.

Ortega froze, his hands on the handles.

Durrie headed toward the controls for the electric motor. "Screw that. We've got to get out of here."

"Don't," Jacko said, glaring at him.

Durrie's hand hovered over the start button.

"That's an order," Jacko hissed.

Durrie hesitated a moment longer before pulling his hand back. "Yes, sir."

"We don't go anywhere until you secure the window."

Until this moment, Durrie had thought of Jacko as just another annoying—but not fatally so—operative. Now, he saw the mission leader for who he really was—yet another in a long line of people actively working against Durrie's interests, part of a growing conspiracy to drive him out of the business or, quite possibly, to see him dead.

If Jacko wanted the window sealed back up, then fine, Durrie would seal it up. But he wasn't going to be stupid about it. From his bag, he withdrew a stethoscope and placed the chest piece against the window.

He heard someone run into the room.

"What is it?" a male voice said.

"He's dead," a second replied. This voice came from closer to the bathroom and matched that of the person Durrie had heard calling for Masiar.

"What? Dead?"

"He's in here."

Durrie heard the two men hurry into the bathroom.

"Jesus. What happened?"

"It…it looks like he slipped."

"Did you check his pulse?"

"Yeah."

In the silence that followed, Durrie imagined the two men examining the body.

Finally the first voice said, "This is way above our pay grade."

"Should we call Novak?"

"Definitely. Let's close this place up. I don't think we should touch anything until he decides what he wants us to do."

The men walked out of the bedroom and closed the door.

Durrie pulled the stethoscope off the glass. "They're gone."

While Ortega held the pane in place, Durrie reattached the outside frame, and filled the gap between the glass and the frame with a fast-drying rubber compound similar in color to that used in the original construction.

Durrie tested the rubber several times until he deemed it hard enough to hold the glass in place.

"Pop them off," he said to Ortega.

Ortega removed the handles but kept them near the glass until he was sure the pane wouldn't fall out. When it looked as though it would stay in place, he returned the handles to the bag.

Durrie turned to Jacko. "Anything else you want to hang around here for, *sir*?"

Jaw tensing, Jacko said, "Take us up."

Once they were on the roof, with no one to hear them, Jacko turned on Durrie, stepping in close so that their chests were almost touching.

"You want to explain yourself?" he asked.

"Explain what?"

"Why you were going to leave me in there!"

"It's not my fault you were slow."

Durrie started to turn away, but Jacko grabbed his arm and

spun him back around. "If they had found me in there, the whole mission would have been blown."

"Their interest was in the bathroom. You could have ducked under the bed until the body was taken away and hidden there."

"Hide under the bed? That's your response?"

Durrie shrugged, pried Jacko's hand off his arm, and walked over to Ortega.

Seething, Jacko said, "You and I are *never* working together again."

"Good. I'd rather work with someone who knew what they were doing anyway."

Jacko turned on his comm. "Assembly point. Three minutes. We're pulling out." He walked toward the roof access door without looking back.

Durrie said to Ortega, "Good job down there."

"Thank you," Ortega said. He looked toward Jacko's receding back. "What's that guy's problem?"

"An ego that doesn't match up to his abilities. Grab the stuff. Let's get out of here."

3

SAN DIEGO, CALIFORNIA

Durrie flew to LAX the next morning, where he grabbed a connector to San Diego, and arrived home just after seven p.m.

He had spent a good portion of the trip stewing about Jacko, and coming up with devious ways to screw with the operative's life. He found himself doing that a lot recently, with many different people. He'd even taken action on several similar fantasies over the past eighteen months, with no regrets, only satisfaction. After all, each and every one of them had wronged him in one way or another and deserved what they got.

Durrie was a legend in the business, the best damn cleaner the secret world had ever seen. *Would* ever see, in fact. At one time, respect from his "peers" had been automatic. It still should have been, but no, people treated him like a child now, questioning his every move, and getting in his face like Jacko had, when they really should have been bowing down in thanks that they had the chance to work with him.

He could pinpoint the moment when the wolves had turned on him.

It had been after a job to take out a low-level Iranian agent, in Mumbai, India, twenty months earlier. A car accident on the way to the mission location, a few minutes of unconsciousness, and then recriminations from both the ops leader and the client that the job had gone south because Durrie hadn't been able to make it to the site on time.

None of it was his fault. Not the accident, not the bump on his head, not someone finding the body before he could get there. But that didn't matter. It's what the others chose to believe that became reality.

Durrie had always been jaded to a certain extent. He'd long ago told himself it was what helped him be so good at his job. But after Mumbai, his contempt for the world he worked in grew exponentially. Alongside this, an anger at his unfair treatment began to build inside him.

And as if his colleagues turning against him wasn't enough, not long after the Mumbai job, he started experiencing migraines once or twice a month. These served to heighten his resentment of those out to get him. Thankfully, he was able to hide the headaches from everyone, including Orlando. If his enemies had known, he knew they would've used the migraines as another means of discrediting him. And if Orlando had known, she would have insisted he see a doctor. He didn't need a doctor. He actually liked the pain. It was one of the few things he could really feel.

In the months that followed, he'd wondered if he should even care anymore. If there were forces out to destroy him, why should he worry about how good of a job he did, when all he really needed to do was just enough? The answer, he soon realized, was he shouldn't care.

To hell with everyone else, he'd decided. From that point onward, he would care only about himself.

He had no doubt Jacko was one of the bastards who wanted Durrie kicked to the curb, and that the ops leader's mission report to Peter—head of the Office, and the client on the Honolulu job— would reflect this.

Durrie had been freelancing for the Office for a lot longer than most operatives had even been in the business, and he had built up a considerable amount of trust. He could count on Peter, and Peter could count on Durrie.

Several months ago, however, Peter had begun questioning Durrie's performances, even going as far as accusing him—more than once—of failing to live up to his abilities. That was when Durrie realized Peter had started to buy into the rumors about Durrie. During Durrie's last conversation with the Office's director, Peter had said, "You keep screwing up like this and you can look for work elsewhere."

And now, Jacko could torpedo Durrie's career.

I should probably get ahead of this, Durrie thought. *Submit my own version of events before Peter has time to digest Jacko's drivel.*

Durrie's would be the correct version, naturally, where he would explain how he had thought Jacko was already on the scaffolding, and when he realized the assassin wasn't, it was with extreme reluctance that he had ordered Ortega to seal the window. No one was happier than he was when Jacko had appeared before it was too late. Durrie would even suggest Peter talk to Ortega. Ortega would back him up. The guy owed everything he had in the business to Durrie.

But every time Durrie thought about what he should write, he became angrier and angrier. Why should he have to justify himself to Peter? Their history was long and deep. If Peter had questions, he could ask Durrie. And if Peter couldn't see through the garbage Jacko was spewing, so be it. The Office wouldn't deserve Durrie's talents, and he'd find work elsewhere.

What he conveniently chose not to dwell on was the fact that work from other agencies had all but dried up over the last year.

Those were just bumps in the road, caused by extenuating circumstances he had no control over.

The jobs would come.

They always did.

He picked up his car from long-term parking and drove to the house he shared with his girlfriend, Orlando. For a few minutes, he was happy to be headed home, but soon his mind began churning again, devolving his mood once more.

He could see his arrival in his mind.

Orlando would be waiting for him, smiling.

She would hug him and kiss him and tell him to have a seat while she grabbed him a beer.

As he settled on the couch and took a drink, she would massage his shoulders.

Then, at some point, she would ask the magic question: "How did it go?"

Only that's not really what she would be asking. Hidden within her innocuous words would be other questions like "Were there any problems?" and "Did you piss anyone off again?" and "When's the next job?"

A man should be happy to return to his home. He should be able to walk in, sit down, and not talk if he didn't want to. He shouldn't have to explain himself to the woman who was supposed to love him.

Maybe she's not home, he thought.

He hadn't told her specifically when he would return, just sometime that evening. Perhaps she assumed he wouldn't be arriving until nine or ten or, please God, even eleven, and had gone to a movie. A few hours in the house alone would do wonders for him.

He imagined their place, empty and quiet, and held tightly to the thought as he turned onto their street.

The sun had yet to set, so he couldn't tell if any lights were on in the house. Still hopeful, he turned into the driveway and activated the remote to open the two-car garage.

Before the door had moved more than a third of the way up, his stomach clenched.

Parked inside was Orlando's car.

"She could have gone out with a friend who picked her up," he mumbled.

He pulled into his spot and sat for a moment in the cooling

car, wanting to calm down before he went inside. He was, at best, marginally successful, but if he didn't go in soon, she would come looking for him. And if that happened, it would only inflame him.

He climbed out, retrieved his bag from the backseat, and entered the house.

Orlando was not in the dining area, waiting. She wasn't in the kitchen or the living room, either. The sliding glass door to the backyard was open, and he could hear familiar, rhythmic thuds.

He walked over and stepped outside.

Orlando was at the other end of their covered porch, decked out in workout clothes, and kicking the heavy punching bag that hung from the ceiling.

She looked over and smiled. "Welcome home."

After giving the bag one more kick, she jogged over, hugged him, and kissed him softly on the lips.

When she let go, she asked, "How was the flight?"

"Fine."

They moved back in the house.

"Tired?"

"No more than usual."

She smiled again, and while it looked innocent, he wondered what she was really thinking.

She picked up his suitcase and carried it toward their bedroom in the back of the house. "There's beer in the fridge," she called as she disappeared.

"Now I have to get it myself?" he muttered.

He found a Sam Adams in the refrigerator and popped the top. What he needed was the burn that came from crappy whiskey, but the beer would have to do.

He took a swig, not bothering to pour it into a glass, and closed his eyes as the liquid rushed down his throat. When he opened them again, Orlando was standing a few feet away, her brow furrowed.

"Are you okay?" she asked.

Whatever small amount of relief the beer had given him vanished. "Sure. Why wouldn't I be okay?"

"It's just...you looked…. Never mind."

"I looked what?"

"Nothing. Forget about it."

"No. Tell me what you were going to say. I looked what?"

She frowned. "You looked...unhappy."

"Why shouldn't I be unhappy? I come in here after a long trip and you start grilling me."

"What are you talking about? I just asked if you were—"

"I know what you asked!"

He closed his eyes again and took a deep breath.

He knew deep down that out of everyone in his life, Orlando was the one still on his side. Not Peter, not any of the bastards he'd worked with. Not even his apprentice—check that, *former* apprentice—Quinn.

He couldn't afford to push Orlando away, but he wasn't particularly fond of apologizing, so he did the best he could. "I… I'm just tired."

She walked over and put a hand against his cheek. The anger he'd been feeling faded. At least for now. He leaned into her palm, drawing in the love she was giving as if it were the answer to all his problems.

"Peter called," she said.

Durrie's eyes snapped open. "What did he want?"

"Said he wanted you to call him when you got home."

He pulled away from her hand. "That's it? Nothing else?"

"Nothing."

"He didn't mention the job?"

"No. Why? Did something happen?"

He searched her face, looking for any indication that Peter had told her. Jacko's version, anyway. But Durrie could see only confusion in her eyes. She was a good actor, though. One of the best. It was one of the qualities that made her an excellent operative in her own right.

"I'm just glad you're back and safe," she said when he didn't respond. "Nothing else matters. Whatever happened, you don't even have to tell—"

"Nothing happened."

"Okay, good. Nothing happened." She smiled. "Why don't you go take a shower? I'll make some dinner. Chicken and penne sound good?"

He took a moment before answering. "Yeah. Fine."

He headed back to their bedroom, closed the door, and tossed his phone on the bed, having no intention of calling Peter.

If the head of the Office wanted to talk to him, he could call again.

———

Orlando waited until she heard their bedroom door close before she pulled out her phone and typed a text to Peter.

He just got home. And I passed on your message.

She moved her thumb to the SEND button, but hesitated. Sure, she'd promised Peter she'd let him know when Durrie got back. But given Durrie's mood, she wasn't sure how long it would be before he returned Peter's call. She didn't want to risk Peter growing angry as he waited for Durrie to call.

She hit DELETE.

To distract herself, she filled a pot with water and put it on the stove. While it heated up, she prepared the vegetables and chicken.

In her chest, the ball of worry that had become her constant companion of late felt as though it had doubled in size since she'd talked to Peter that morning.

He'd told her how Durrie had disregarded the life of another team member and put the mission in jeopardy. She'd wanted to say she didn't believe it, but she couldn't muster the words because she knew he was telling the truth.

"I can't afford what might happen if I put him on another job," Peter said.

"Please, just one more chance. You owe him that much."

"I don't know if I owe him a damn thing anymore."

"Please, Peter. Then do it for me. One more time. If he botches that one up, I'll never ask again."

Peter was silent for several seconds. "*If* I give him another job, there will be conditions."

"Of course. Whatever you want."

More silence. "There is something coming up next week that I *might* be able to put him on. But, Orlando, he won't be lead. He'll be number two."

"Who-who would be lead?"

"Quinn."

"Quinn?" She paused. "Actually, that's a great idea. It would be good for them to work together again. It's been a while. And Quinn could…keep him on the right track."

"That's what I would be hoping. But I can't imagine Durrie playing second to his own apprentice."

"Please, ask him. He'll probably say no at first, but I'll work on him from my end. I'll convince him. I promise."

She heard Peter take a deep breath. "I know I'm going to regret this."

"You won't. Please, Peter."

Another pause. "Tell him to call me when he gets home."

"Thank you. Thank you so much."

"Don't thank me yet. If he pisses me off during the call, he's out."

"He won't."

Peter snorted. "Text me when he gets there, so I can be… mentally prepared for when he calls."

"Sure. No problem."

She sliced up a zucchini, three bell peppers, and an onion, and removed the fat from two deboned chicken breasts.

On the stove, the water was boiling, so she dumped in the penne and began sautéing the vegetables and meat.

While she may have staved off—at least temporarily—Durrie losing his main source of income, she knew his problems with Peter were symptoms of something else.

Whether mental or physical, something was definitely wrong with Durrie. There was no ignoring the fact the man she had fallen for was not the same one taking a shower right now. Sure, Durrie had always had rough edges, but there had also been a tenderness that was surprisingly deep. She was one of the few who'd ever witnessed that side of him, but she *had* witnessed it. She wasn't seeing any of it now. It was as if the only person Durrie cared about now was himself.

She wasn't sure when the change had occurred. It had been a gradual thing she hadn't realized was happening until far later than she should have. When she did, she'd suggested they go in for couples counseling, thinking his moodiness had something to do with their relationship. He assured her they were fine, that everything was fine.

But whatever was troubling him had only worsened.

The bedroom door opened, and a few seconds later Durrie appeared at the end of the hall, wearing a T-shirt and his favorite sweatpants, his hair tousled from drying.

"It's almost ready," she said. "Grab another beer if you want. Get me one, too."

He entered the kitchen, but instead of opening the refrigerator, he moved in behind her and wrapped his arms around her.

"I don't deserve you," he said.

She hesitated only a second before responding the way she always did. "No, you don't."

"Then why do you hang around?"

"Oh, I don't know. Probably because I love you."

He turned her around and pressed her against the stove.

"Careful. You'll catch us both on fire," she said.

He kissed her, hard and deep, in a way he hadn't in a long, long time. It caught her off guard, but soon enough she responded in kind.

He flipped off the burners and lifted her into his arms, an easy task given her five-foot, ninety-nine-pound frame.

As he carried her out of the kitchen, she said, "What about dinner?"

"It can wait."

In the bedroom, they made love for the first time in months.

And for the last time ever.

4

"I'm sorry, you've tied my hands," Peter said over the phone.

"Only because you're believing that bastard and not me," Durrie said.

He'd waited until the next morning to return Peter's call, after Orlando had gone on a run. He'd prepped himself for Peter letting him go, but that had not happened. What Peter was offering, though, was almost worse.

"Jacko's not the only one who's voiced concerns and you know it," Peter said. "You need to earn back my confidence. You do this and everything goes well, we'll do another one."

"With me still as number two?"

"You prove to me that you can handle that, and that you're not a risk, and we can talk about moving you back to being lead. Eventually."

Durrie scoffed.

"I'm offering you a way out here. So, what's it going to be? Yes or no?"

"You're offering me crap."

"Is that a no?"

Durrie closed his eyes. Being demoted to the number-two position was humiliating enough. Putting his former apprentice, his protégé, in the lead position was soul crushing. If not for Orlando and her belief in him, he would have told Peter to go to hell.

"No, it's not a no. I'll...I'll do it."

"Wow. Can't say that I'm not surprised, but all right. I'll be in touch."

Durrie put his phone in his pocket and looked out the window.

This world was really starting to suck.

5

"Truant for Quinn."

"Go for Quinn."

"Phase one complete."

"Copy, phase one complete," Jonathan Quinn said.

"I'm out. Good luck."

"Pleasure doing business with you."

A double click over the comm from Andreas Truant, echoing the sentiment.

Quinn glanced at Steve Howard, his number two on this mission. "Ready?"

"I'm right behind you."

Quinn led the way out of the basement machine room, past the laundry room, and into the residential stairwell. The muffled sounds of televisions and conversations drifted down the second-floor hallway as they passed the landing and continued up. On the third, they stopped.

More sounds here, though only about half as much as below. Perhaps those who lived on this level were of the early-to-bed variety.

Quinn made sure no one was out in the hall before heading

down to apartment 307. As expected, Truant had left the front door unlocked.

Quinn and Howard found the target slumped over the glass dining room table, head lying on an open newspaper. On the floor next to the man sat an expensive-looking briefcase, the target's initials engraved on the metal plate beneath the handle.

The method of execution had been the introduction of a small-caliber bullet to the back of the target's head, the projectile powerful enough to enter the brain cavity but not escape the skull after it rattled around inside. Because of the way the man had slumped, most of his blood remained inside his body. This was not by accident but a testament to Truant's assassin skills.

Quinn examined the scene, identifying every spot of blood and pointing each out to Howard. After the assessment was completed, he and his number two set to work.

First up: placing a gauze-lined beanie over the man's head and securing it with a roll of self-adherent compression bandage so that no additional blood would leak out. They then laid out the body bag and transferred the target into it.

Next, using a specially crafted solvent, they cleaned up the blood that had made it onto the table and the area around it. The mixture had been developed years earlier by Quinn's mentor, Durrie, and was designed to remove not only visible signs of blood, but also nearly ninety percent of the residue that could be revealed by a UV light. In this particular instance, with such a small amount of splatter, it was unlikely there would be hints of blood left.

Of course it would be weeks, at least, before the target's associates conducted a detailed search of the place. This was the target's private little getaway, an apartment not even his wife knew about. A place where he could unwind and secretly enjoy the teenage boys he liked to pick up. Not a great look for the leader of the Southern Germany Aryan Resurgence.

Well, not a great look for anyone.

By the time the apartment would finally be linked to him, his regularly scheduled maid service would have cleaned the place at least twice, further obscuring any potential evidence Quinn might have missed. Not that he ever missed anything.

This was only the third time Quinn had worked with Howard, and like on the other two jobs, he was pleased with what he saw. Howard was smart, efficient, and reliable. He also wasn't a big talker. Quinn had worked with operatives who would go on and on about nothing at all. Howard's economy of language was appreciated.

Another bonus was that Howard didn't have a problem working for a cleaner, unlike many other operatives who considered what Quinn did beneath them. They preferred jobs that "got more action."

It was a lame excuse. While body removal didn't *sound* glamorous, it was surprising how much action Quinn had been involved in, first during his time as an apprentice, and then over the last few years when working on his own.

While Howard wiped off the other surfaces in the room to remove any stray smudges and markings, Quinn searched the rest of the apartment. The mission brief had doubted anything of value was there, but it had requested a look around nonetheless.

Turned out there was something, after all. Beneath false flooring in the bedroom, Quinn found a safe. Inside were not only files containing information on the target's Aryan brothers, but also a thick manila envelope filled with pictures of some of the boys to whom he had played host.

Quinn flipped through the pictures to make sure nothing was hidden among them. Nothing was, but in addition to shots of the teens, Quinn discovered dozens of photos of other adult males taking part in the…activities.

Though Quinn's mission was being run through the Office, Peter was playing middle man for the job's true client, the BfV, Germany's domestic intelligence agency. Quinn had no doubt the ministry in Cologne would be eager to identify all of the target's friends.

He put the safe's contents into a thick plastic bag and shoved it inside the body bag for easy transport.

He and Howard did a final sweep of the flat, and last but not least, Quinn ran a handheld vacuum over the area where the assassination had taken place, to remove any remaining DNA evidence.

He checked his watch. It was just after eleven p.m. They could probably make it out of the building now without being seen, but there was no reason to risk it. They weren't in a hurry.

"Shall we see what's on TV?" Quinn asked.

At 1:45 a.m., Quinn and Howard carried the body down to the ground level, where Quinn eased open a ground-floor door and peeked into the hallway that led from the building's front lobby.

The corridor was empty.

Quinn motioned for Howard to remain with the body, and then slipped through the opening. This was the most dangerous portion of the mission. The building had a two-man night security team. As long as both remained at the lobby desk, everything would be fine. Quinn needed to make sure they were there.

As he neared the front, he heard voices and music coming from a TV. He stopped just shy of the end of the hall, lowered himself onto his hands and knees, and edged his head out far enough to see the guard desk.

It faced the front of the building, away from him. Behind it were both guards, their attention on a movie playing on one of several monitors.

Perfect.

Quinn hurried back to the stairwell, then he and Howard carried their burden toward the back end of the hall, to a door labeled ZUTRITT FÜR UNBEFUGTE VERBOTEN—entry prohibited to unauthorized persons. The door was locked, but Quinn had procured a key in the lead-up to the evening's activities.

Holding on to his end of the body bag with one hand and balancing the target's shoulder on his knee, Quinn unlocked the door and slowly pushed it inward. Before it was all the way open, the sound of a chair moving in the lobby drifted down the hall.

Quickly, Quinn and Howard moved the body through the doorway. The room they entered was a large, mostly open space, with shelves to the right containing maintenance products and gear. Besides the door they'd used, there were three others—one to a storage room that, according to the building plans, held mail and packages; one to a bathroom; and one to the outside. If Quinn had already turned off the alarm on the back door, that exit would have been the obvious choice. But the process required free hands and a minute on his laptop, and there was no time for that.

Instead, they hurried to the package room. Quinn tried the maintenance-door key, but though it slipped into the lock, it wouldn't turn. He pulled out his lockpicks, inserted the instruments into the keyhole, and coaxed the tumblers into place. As the last one complied, he heard a key slide into the lock on the hallway door. Quinn opened the package room and they rushed inside, getting the door closed again a second before the other one opened.

After carefully setting the body down, Quinn pressed an ear against the door.

Footsteps moved through the room, clicking across the cement floor. A door opened with a subtle whine. Not a heavy door like the one to the outside, but lighter. The bathroom door. When it shut again, the room fell silent.

Figuring they had a few minutes, Quinn removed his laptop and disarmed the rear exit. Then he pressed his ear against the door again.

The silence continued until the sound of a flushing toilet drifted across the room. Half a minute later, the bathroom door opened and the steps crossed back to the hallway door. As soon as the man was gone, Quinn and Howard carried the body bag out of the package room and exited the building.

Soon they were in their car, headed out of town, toward the grave site they'd prepped the day before.

All things considered, a textbook job.

6

WASHINGTON, DC

"You can go in now," the man behind the desk said.

Quinn set down the copy of *Wired* magazine he'd been flipping through, rose, and walked to the door on the man's right.

The office beyond was surprisingly small given the responsibilities of its occupant. Approximately fifteen feet square, the space was crammed with bookcases and filing cabinets and a beat-up-looking metal desk, behind which sat the balding, height-challenged Peter, director of the Office.

"Sit," Peter said, not looking up from the file he was reading.

Quinn lowered into the guest chair and crossed his legs.

Peter's attention stayed on the file for another full minute before he looked up. "Thanks for coming in." While Quinn knew the sentiment was genuine, the tone, as always, was gruff and rushed.

"It was on my way home."

"So, Munich?"

"In, out. Done."

"No problems?"

"None."

"How was working with Truant?"

This was the first time Quinn had been paired with the assassin. "Easy. Professional. No complaints."

Peter grunted. "He said the same about you."

Quinn didn't reply, though he was pleased. He'd been a full-fledged, independent cleaner for only a few years and was still building his reputation. Endorsements like Truant's would go a long way to helping that.

"And your assistant?" Peter asked.

"Howard? Efficient as always." Quinn frowned. "It's, um, all in my report.'"

"Yeah, I read it. But sometimes people write one thing and say another."

"So…you just called me in to check if my report was accurate?"

"What? No. That job's done. I couldn't give a rat's ass about it anymore."

The response did nothing to quell Quinn's growing confusion. "Then what can I do for you?"

Peter grabbed a file off a pile in the corner of his desk and opened it. "Dammit." He closed it and picked up the next one down the stack. "What the hell?" He looked past Quinn toward the door. "Benjamin! Get in here!"

The man from the other room entered. "Yes, sir?"

"Where's the MC-17 file?"

"Sir?"

"The MC-17 file!" Peter gestured at the stack on his desk. "It was right here before I went to lunch!"

"You told me to put the ones from this morning away and bring you the group for this afternoon."

"I did, didn't I? But what else did I tell you?"

A thought brought a cringe to Benjamin's face. "Leave the file that was on top. I'm sorry, sir. I'll retrieve it right away."

Benjamin hurried out the door.

"He's new, right?" Quinn said.

Peter frowned as he nodded.

Quinn could not remember ever seeing one of Peter's assistants on more than one visit. Clearly, it wasn't an easy job to hold. Not exactly the warm and fuzzy type, Peter demanded a lot from those who worked for him. Too much for some.

He made similar demands on Quinn, too, but that didn't bother Quinn. He liked to work hard.

Given that Benjamin couldn't even remember a small detail in a simple set of instructions, Quinn had no doubt another new face would be sitting at the desk the next time he came around.

The door opened and Benjamin rushed back in and set a file on Peter's desk. "I'm sorry, sir. Completely my mistake. Won't happen again."

Peter stared at him, his face blank.

Benjamin took a backward step toward the door. "Again, I'm very sorry." Another step. "Really."

Peter kept his gaze on his assistant until Benjamin moved across the threshold and shut the door. Peter then opened the file and pulled out a photo.

Setting it on the desk so Quinn could see it, he said, "Felix Ruiz."

The picture was a professional headshot of a man in his late forties or early fifties. He had well-groomed salt-and-pepper hair, and a you-can-trust-me smile.

"Don't tell me," Quinn said. "A lawyer?"

Peter grinned. "Dead on. You're getting good at this."

"Thanks."

"Ruiz works out of Mexico City. Small office, small cases. But that's on purpose, to disguise how he makes his real money."

"And how is that?"

"Laundering cash for the Martinez Cartel in Monterrey."

"Wonderful," Quinn said, frowning. He was a former police officer, and few things pissed him off more than drugs and cartels.

"Mexican authorities caught up to him about six months ago, but instead of putting him away, he agreed to turn informant."

"Oh, okay. That's useful."

Peter winced. "Not as much as you might think. Let's just say he wasn't as sincere as he should have been after he took the deal. Two weeks ago, a pair of undercover agents went missing. Their bodies showed up last weekend. Well, enough of their bodies to be identified, anyway. My client was able to tie their deaths directly to information Ruiz passed on to his employers."

"So, this is a termination mission? Why not just arrest him?"

"As soon as word got out, the cartel would eliminate him. The client would rather be the one directly responsible for Ruiz's demise."

"Demise. Nice word choice. When is this going to happen?"

"You'll leave in four days."

"Okay. Sounds good. But, you know, we could have talked about this over the phone."

Peter tapped the file. "This? This is just background for what I really need to talk to you about."

"And what would that be?"

"I know you prefer to choose your own team, but I'm assigning you your assistant this time."

Quinn's eyes narrowed. "Who?"

"Durrie."

Quinn stared at Peter, not sure he had heard correctly. "Durrie as in my mentor, Durrie?"

"Do you know any others? Because I don't."

"No. So why him?"

Peter sighed then told Quinn about Durrie's behavior as of late, and how Peter had offered him this last chance to get on track.

Quinn was aware something was going on with Durrie. He'd picked it up from conversations with Orlando, though she'd never said as much directly. It was little things pieced together, and things left unsaid. And then there were the rumors from other operatives. But this was the first confirmation he'd received.

"And he's agreed to take the assist position?" Quinn asked.

"He has."

That was a shock. "Does he realize I'm going to lead?"

"He does."

"And he still said yes?"

"Uh-huh."

This was even more surprising. "In essence, you're asking me to be his babysitter, right?"

"I need someone there who can keep things on track."

"And if he screws up again?"

"Then he'll never work for the Office again."

Which meant Durrie would likely be done working for anyone of consequence.

"What if he doesn't screw up?" Quinn asked.

"I'll try him on another job. With you as lead again."

"Do I have any say in this?"

"You can say no. And if you do, I'll call him and tell him the deal's off. He's done."

Son of a bitch. Quinn understood Peter's reasoning in making Quinn's involvement a requirement, but he hated being put in the middle of this. What was he going to do, though—turn his back on his mentor? He owed Durrie too much to do that.

"All right, fine. I'll do it."

"Good. I'll send you the information, and I look forward to reading your end-of-mission report."

7

SAN DIEGO

The tension had returned.

It'd started the morning after Durrie came back from Hawaii. He'd risen before Orlando, and when she wandered into the kitchen twenty minutes later, she'd found him sitting at the dining table, already in a mood.

She'd filled cups of coffee for both of them, set his on the table near him, and headed back to the master bathroom to take a shower, all without saying a word. Sometimes it was better to let him stew for a while and work out whatever was bothering him. Sometimes that didn't even work.

When she returned, he looked at her and said, "Well, I'm not fired," and that was when she realized he'd finally called Peter.

"Of course you're not. He would have been a fool to let you go."

A grunt was his only response.

Over the remainder of the day, he revealed bits and pieces of his conversation with the Office's director. Orlando was careful not to ask any questions that would reveal she'd known about Peter's offer ahead of time. She merely acted the supportive girlfriend, happy he still had work, and sympathetic with his annoyance at the restrictions placed on him.

The next day hadn't been any better, making her concerned that if he didn't get his head straightened out, he would screw up again. Try as she might, though, her efforts to soothe his resentment had met with little success.

On the third day, Quinn called her.

"I've been trying to reach Durrie," he said. "He's not answering."

"Oh, um, he probably just has his phone off," she said. "He does that sometimes."

Durrie had left that morning with little more than "I'll be back later." And while it was true he did sometimes switch off his phone, she had a feeling that wasn't the reason he'd failed to pick up when Quinn called.

"I need to talk to him. We're doing a job together." A pause. "You know about that, right?"

"Yeah. He mentioned it the other day."

"We leave in two days and I need to brief him."

"I'll-I'll make sure he gives you a call back."

"Thanks. I appreciate that." The line fell silent for a moment. "How are you doing?"

"Me? Oh, um, I'm fine," she replied, trying to match her tone to her words. "How about you?"

"Everything's good here. Have you been working?"

"You know, on and off." Her assignments had been spotty, but not because the offers hadn't come. As Durrie seemed to be getting worse, she took only jobs that allowed her to be home when he was, so she could help him through what she hoped was only a temporary rough patch.

"We should, uh, get together sometime," Quinn said. "Maybe after this job? You know, catch up?"

"That sounds great." It did. Quinn was her best friend, even more so than Durrie. But since she and Durrie had moved to San Diego, the opportunities to hang out with Quinn had decreased dramatically.

"Cool."

An awkward silence. It was all Orlando could to do to keep from confiding in Quinn about everything that was going on. He knew a little, of course, from previous conversations, but she had never revealed the true depth of Durrie's issues.

In the end, she did what she always did—keep the pain to herself. "I'll, uh, see if I can track down Durrie and get him to call you."

"I appreciate it."

"Talk to you later."

"Definitely."

She tried calling Durrie, but after two rings was sent to voice mail.

Though he hadn't told her where he was going, she had a pretty good idea of where that was.

The drive to the Tin Star Bar in Oceanside took her thirty minutes. Sure enough, Durrie's car was parked in the dirt lot beside the cinderblock building. She pulled in next to it and called his cell again. This time it didn't even ring before the prerecorded message kicked in.

She sat in her car, staring at the building. She didn't want to go inside. It would only rile him up. But what choice did she have? If she didn't go get him, he'd stay at the bar all day and not even think about contacting Quinn. And if that happened, Quinn would be forced to let Peter know.

Then that would be that. Durrie would be out for good.

She took several deep breaths to psyche herself up and climbed out of her car.

The Tin Star was a dive bar, frequented by retired marine vets who lived in Oceanside to be close to Camp Pendleton. No officers, enlisted men only. Like Durrie had been right out of high school over three decades ago. Occasionally there were a few females around, but not often. It was a boys' bar, where boys came to tell tales of their youth, give voice to the offenses done to them, and expound on what they would do if they had the power. Not exactly a pleasant place for someone like her.

Thankfully, the front door led into a vestibule and not directly into the bar, so she was able to take a few moments to let her eyes adjust to the low lighting before anyone noticed her. When she was ready, she slipped into the main room and stood just inside, searching for Durrie.

Though it was midday on a Thursday, at least two dozen people were spread throughout the room. Seating at the bar was full, while the rest of the day drinkers were scattered among the tables.

It didn't take long for her to spot her boyfriend. He sat at the bar between two fat, gray-haired men, all three of them nursing beers and not talking to one another.

She'd taken only ten steps into the room when the first patron noticed her.

"This day just got a lot better," the guy said from his table.

She kept walking without a glance in his direction. She expected him to follow it up with a crude remark, but he said nothing else.

Others were not quite as kind. Once they realized a woman was in their midst, out came the offers of free drinks and available chairs.

While it was annoying, she didn't respond. All that would do was encourage them. Besides, she'd heard worse in her life. All women had. She did allow herself, however, to fantasize about how long it would take her to beat the crap out of every single person in the room.

Two minutes. Tops.

Durrie didn't turn and look at her until she was standing beside him. He sighed and said, "You want a drink?"

"No."

"It's a bar, babe. That's what people come here for."

She was trying very hard to keep her anger in check, but a little leaked into her voice. "You're not answering your phone."

"Because I'm busy."

"Quinn needs to talk to you."

He turned back to the bar, picked up his beer, and took a drink without saying anything.

Orlando leaned forward and whispered into his ear, "He needs to brief you about Saturday."

"Are you not listening to me? I'm busy."

"You agreed to do this job."

"So what?"

"What do you mean, so what? Are you backing out?"

"Did you hear me say that? No, you didn't." He took another swallow. "All I said was that I'm busy right now."

She leaned back. "And how long will you be *busy*?"

He shrugged. "Can't say. A while, I suppose. Now, if you're not going to drink with me, you can go back home."

She had never been so close to telling him she was leaving him. She barely recognized him anymore. Something was seriously wrong, but as much as her anger was telling her to walk away, she wasn't ready to give up on him.

Not yet.

"Give me your keys," she said.

"What?" he said, brow furrowing.

She held out her hand. "Your keys. If you're going to drink all day, you're not driving home. You can call me when you're done and I'll come pick you up."

He stared across the bar for a few seconds, then pulled out his keys and dumped them in her hand. "Don't wait up. I'll get a cab."

———

"Hi, it's me," Orlando said into her phone. She was still in her car but back in San Diego, parked in her garage.

"Hey," Quinn said. "What's up?"

"So, um, I think there must be something wrong with Durrie's phone. We'll make sure it gets taken care of before he meets up with you, but I thought maybe it would save time if you gave me the download and I filled him in when he got back."

She knew what she was asking was a breach of protocol, but it was the only thing she could think of doing to ensure Durrie was ready to travel on Saturday.

Quinn didn't say anything for a moment, making her think he wasn't willing to step over the line. She instantly regretted asking him. She was putting him in a terrible place.

Maybe…it would be better if she let Durrie fail. It seemed inevitable, anyway.

"I guess that would be okay," Quinn said.

And like that, Orlando's despair turned back to hope.

He gave her a basic outline of the mission, ending with, "On Saturday, we fly out of LAX. Aeromexico at 5:25 p.m. I need him there by three."

"Don't worry. I'll make sure of it. Anything else?"

"No, that should do it."

"Thanks, Quinn. I appreciate it."

A slight pause, then, "You know I'm always here for you."

Durrie didn't get home until one a.m. There was no sense in telling him then what Quinn had said.

After he passed out, Orlando lay awake for another hour, her mind racing. Historically, Durrie was not a heavy drinker. Sure, there had been some hard nights out in his past, but since she had moved in with him, his pattern had been a beer or two, maybe a glass of wine a few times a week. Even his visits to the Tin Star had occurred only once or twice a month at most, and wouldn't go beyond three beers.

Recently, however, those trips to the bar had increased to several times a week, with a definite uptick in the number of drinks. Even by those standards, tonight's incident was unprecedented. He had been there for over twelve hours, and God only knew how many beers he had drunk. She hoped it was an aberration but feared it was the new norm.

Let him get through this job. If things go well, he'll find his way back to normal.

I know he will.

———

When Orlando woke the next morning, she was alone.

She raced through the house, looking everywhere for him. When she couldn't find him, she checked the garage, thinking he had taken her car. But it was still there.

She told herself he had probably gone out for a walk. A little exercise after a day of drinking. She purposely didn't check the drawer where she'd put his keys, wanting to believe they were still there. But when ninety minutes had passed and he hadn't shown up, she could no longer put it off.

The keys were gone. Which meant he must have taken a cab back to the Tin Star.

She drove there, still dressed in the gym shorts and T-shirt she'd thrown on when she woke. His car sat in the same spot it had been in the previous day. She went inside, but this time she didn't go past the entry hall. A peek around the corner allowed her to see him, sitting in the same seat, downing another beer.

Not wanting to make a scene, she went back outside and disabled his car, by cutting the wires to the fuel pump.

She spent the afternoon at home, researching rehab facilities. She knew there was little chance he would agree to enter one, but she wanted to be ready in the unlikely chance he said yes.

That evening, as she sat at the dining table, waiting for Durrie to return, Quinn called.

"Just wanted to make sure Durrie didn't have any questions," he said.

"Nope. He's all good."

Quinn paused. "Should I be looking for a backup?"

"No, of course not. He'll be there. You can count on it."

"If you're sure."

"I am."

Another pause, then, "Okay. Tell him I'll meet him at the gate."

"Quinn, thank you."

"I haven't done anything."

"You have. And I appreciate it. Safe travels."

Midnight came, and no Durrie.

One a.m.

Then two.

It was ten minutes to three when lights lit up the front of their house. Orlando hurried to the door and opened it. She knew she should wait but couldn't help herself.

In the driveway, Durrie was slowly extracting himself from a taxi. Once out, he weaved his way along the stone path to the front door, not noticing her standing on the porch until he was a few feet away. He jerked in surprise.

"Are you all right?" she asked.

"I'm fine. Why wouldn't I be?"

He pushed past her into the house.

"You do realize you have a flight leaving for LAX in eight hours, don't you?"

As he headed across the living room toward the hallway, he said, "I'm not going."

"Excuse me?"

He paused and looked back. "You heard me. Tell Quinn I'm...I don't know, sick or something. I don't care, whatever. I have plans tomorrow."

"You have plans to go to Mexico City!"

"Not gonna happen, baby." He turned to walk away.

"Goddammit, I promised him you'd be there!"

Without stopping, he said, "Did I tell you to do that? No, I didn't, did I? You should have asked me first."

The bedroom door slammed shut, leaving Orlando staring at the space where Durrie had been.

8

Quinn checked his watch again. It was almost 3:30 p.m. and no sign of Durrie.

He'd tried calling his mentor, but like in the past few days, his calls went straight to voice mail. He'd tried Orlando, too, but was also shuffled off to message land.

"Dammit," he muttered.

He should have listened to his instincts and put someone else on hold. Hopefully, there was an op in the Mexico City area who could jump in on a moment's notice. If not, Quinn would have to do the gig by himself. A difficult task, but not impossible.

His stomach rumbled.

He'd give Durrie five more minutes, then he'd go in search of food.

He was so focused on looking for his mentor that he didn't notice the slight Asian woman walking toward him.

"Quinn?"

He blinked as he realized it was Orlando. "What are you doing here?" He looked around. "Where's Durrie?"

"He's, um, not coming. Something came up last minute. I didn't want to leave you without any help so I'm here to fill in."

The first emotion Quinn should have felt was anger, but it

wasn't. What he felt instead was relief. Ever since Peter had presented him with the task of being Durrie's minder, Quinn had worried something would go awry, and he'd be forced to torpedo the career of the man who'd given Quinn this life. Now, knowing he wouldn't have to constantly look over his shoulder to supervise Durrie took a massive load off his shoulders. Throw in the fact he'd be spending the next couple of days with Orlando, and the job he had been dreading was now something he was looking forward to.

"Is he okay?" Quinn asked.

"He…will be."

Quinn paused. While it was a relief Durrie had backed out, Quinn would still need to inform Peter, which would mean the end of Durrie's career. "I'll…need to put why in my report."

Orlando looked around. "How about we sit?"

She led him over to Gate 28, where a flight had just departed, leaving the area all but empty. They took two seats facing the window.

"I know I'm not in a position to do this, but I need to ask you for a favor," she said.

"Of course. What is it?" There were three people in the world he would do anything for—his estranged sister, Liz, and Orlando were two of them, and he hadn't talked to Liz in several years. His mother came in a close third, but certain conditions were attached there.

"I'd like you to not tell Peter," she said.

"I'm not…sure how I can do that. Durrie's not here. Peter needs to know that."

"The only ones who need to know he didn't make it are you and me. As far as anyone else is concerned, he's on the job."

Quinn sat back, unsure how to respond.

Orlando leaned close to him. "I realize this is a huge ask, but this could be Durrie's last chance. I don't know how much Peter told you, but Durrie's on this job with you because—"

"He told me everything."

"Oh. I see. Well, um, good. Then you understand. If you tell Peter, Durrie is done." She took a breath. "This is his *life*. If he doesn't have this, then I don't know what he'll do."

"He's the one who put himself in this position."

"I realize that. And he probably doesn't deserve a second chance, but I'm trying to help him through this. Get him back to where he was."

"Through what exactly?"

Her shoulders sagged and her head dipped. "Whatever is going on in his head."

"You don't know what's wrong with him?"

"I'm...not sure." After a beat, she puffed up a bit. "But I'm going to get him through this. I promise. I just need you to do this one thing for me." Another pause. "If you can't, I'll understand. I'll still help you with this job, then Durrie and I will figure our way through whatever's next."

Quinn realized if he refused her request, their relationship would never be the same. And while they might work together now and then, the closeness they'd had, the trust, would be gone. Whatever his thoughts were about helping Durrie, not having Orlando in his life anymore was not something he could live with. Though she'd probably never know it, she was everything to him.

"Okay," he said. "We'll keep it between us."

The words were barely past his lips when she pulled him into a hug and whispered in his ear, "Thank you."

"If anyone else on the job finds out, or something goes wrong, I'll have to come clean."

"I know. We'll just have to make sure none of those things happen."

SAN DIEGO

After a lunch of tacos from the takeout place down the block from the Tin Star, Durrie, who had yet to drink enough to cloud his mind, came down with a case of the guilts.

Peter may have been a son of a bitch, but he *had* thrown Durrie a lifeline. The fact that Durrie had let go of it could be blamed on no one but himself.

"Shit," he said, setting down his barely touched beer. He waved at Garner, the bartender. "What do I owe you?"

Getting his car working again was a lot easier to do since he was more sober than he'd been the previous night. When he arrived home, he was surprised to find Orlando's car gone. Lately she'd made it a point to wait around for him. Maybe she'd finally given up. He wouldn't blame her if she did.

He headed to the back of the house, where he retrieved his laptop, and carried it to the dining table. His plan was to arrange for the soonest flight he could get to Mexico City from San Diego, but before he could set the computer down, he saw a piece of paper lying at his usual spot.

He picked it up, sure it was Orlando's long overdue Dear John letter. Only that's not what it was.

D—

Have gone to LAX to take your place on the job. If I can work it so that Peter doesn't find out, I will. That way you'll still have another chance. I don't know what's going on with you, but you need to pull it together. If not for yourself, do it for me. Please.

I'll be back in a few days. I love you.
O.

He stared at the paper, his eyes narrowing.

There Orlando went again, playing the hero girlfriend. And who was she enlisting in her quest to "clear" Durrie's name? His own ungrateful apprentice.

Or maybe that had been her plan all along. Maybe she had

counted on Durrie dropping out so she and Quinn could have an all-expenses-paid trip to Mexico.

He could feel a burning at the base of his skull, a burning that told him his suspicions might very well be correct.

No. *Were* correct.

Slowly he wadded up the lying piece of paper and tossed it in the trash can. He headed out to his car, his guilt no longer an issue.

EN ROUTE TO MEXICO CITY, MEXICO

Quinn stared at the open book in his hand. He had no idea how many times he'd tried to read the same page. Four? Five? More? Every time, after only a few lines, his thoughts had wandered to the head resting against his shoulder.

"Tired?" he'd asked, when Orlando yawned after he'd agreed to her plan.

"No. Just had to get up a little early, to take care of a few things before I left."

The denial was a lie. Exhaustion lay heavy across her eyes, her lids sagging as if their new position had become permanent.

Five minutes after their flight reached cruising altitude, she had passed out. And not long after that, her body slid sideways against his, where it had remained ever since.

He had done his best to ignore her presence and not think about her. He'd actually succeeded for a while. Now that they were nearing Mexico City and she would soon be waking, he gave up even trying.

More than anything, he wanted to reach over and stroke her cheek. He wanted to push up the armrest separating them and let her lie in his lap. He wanted to put his arms around her and tell her it was all going to be okay.

But none of those options were open to him. All he could do was stare at his book, unable to understand a word.

He had loved her for years, and yet she was not his to love. That honor belonged to the man responsible for her exhaustion.

Quinn grimaced.

Obviously Durrie was taking out his issues on her. Quinn couldn't understand how in God's name Durrie could do that. Orlando had done nothing but defend Durrie. She had even roped in Quinn to cover up Durrie's absence. She deserved Durrie's deep appreciation and thanks, not whatever psychological BS he was radiating.

Maybe I should have refused to go along with her plan, he thought. Maybe what Durrie needed was to finally crash and burn. He could either rise from the ashes a reborn man or disappear into the debris, never to be seen again. Either way, it would give Orlando a chance to start anew.

But even if Quinn could have said no to her—which was doubtful—it was too late to say it now. They were in this together, charter members of Team Rescue Durrie from Himself.

Crap.

The lights in the cabin brightened, and a *dong* rang out over the intercom system.

Over the speaker, a flight attendant announced, first in Spanish and then in English, "Ladies and gentlemen, we are about to begin our descent into Mexico City. At this time, please stow your tray tables and return your chairs to their upright position."

Orlando took a deep breath and slowly opened her eyes. When she realized she was leaning against him, she didn't immediately pull away, but lingered there for a few moments before leaning back into her own seat.

"Sorry," she said. "I didn't mean to knock out like that."

"Don't worry about it," he said.

"I take it you slept, too, huh?"

"What?"

She nodded at his book. "Doesn't look like you got very far."

His finger held a place only a handful of pages from the beginning of the book. "Yeah, a little, I guess," he lied.

The plane landed without incident. Because of the time change between California and Mexico City, by the time they were through Customs and Immigration and climbing into a taxi, it was almost midnight.

Peter had arranged for a studio apartment, not for its comfort but due to its location, close to the mission site but not too close—a vital factor given the notorious Mexico City traffic. The single room was filled with a small table, two chairs, a pullout sofa, and one full-sized bed. The only privacy was the small attached bathroom.

The place would have been fine if Durrie had been with Quinn, but not so much now. They couldn't change locations, though. That would mean coming up with another lie to tell Peter.

"You can have the bed. I'll take the couch," Quinn said.

She walked over to the sofa, pulled off one of the cushions, and checked the mattress. "This thing's only a few inches thick. You'll be up all night."

"I can sleep on the cushions. It'll be fine."

She snorted. "You're about a half foot too tall."

"Okay, fine. You take the couch."

"Oh, hell, no. I'm not sleeping on this, and neither are you."

He blinked. "I, um, I guess I could sleep on the floor."

"For God's sake. And how is that going to give you a decent night's sleep?" She shook her head, looking at him as if he were an idiot. "We've got work tomorrow. We both have to be on top of our game. We can share the bed."

"Really, you don't need to—"

"I'm not arguing about this with you anymore. If it helps with your moral dilemma, choirboy, I trust you. Okay?"

"Well, um, okay, sure."

Technically, this wasn't the first time they'd slept together. It wasn't even the second or third. Back when they were both apprentices working on the same gig, they'd catch a few winks when they could, wherever they could. The major difference was, none of those other times had ever been on a bed.

At Orlando's insistence, Quinn used the bathroom first. After he came out and she went in, he pulled on his running shorts and a clean T-shirt, and climbed into bed on the side farthest from the bathroom.

When she came out, she too was wearing a T-shirt, only hers fit like a loose dress that came down to her thighs. She turned off the light and made her way to the bed by the glow of the street-lights outside the window.

As she crawled in beside him, she said, "If I kick you, don't take it personally. It just means you're hogging too much space and you need to move."

Quinn and Orlando had spent years joking with each other so he knew she was being funny, but for the first time in as long as he could remember, he couldn't come up with a better comeback than "Yes, ma'am."

She squirmed a little, getting comfortable, and moved the pillow around until it was just right.

"Did you set an alarm?" she asked.

"Six a.m."

"Ugh, that's going to come quick. All right. Good night, honey."

Before he could stop himself, he let out a surprised "What?"

"Oh, I'm sorry. Do you prefer sweetheart? How about lover? Sounds so romance novel-y, doesn't it? Lover." She laughed. "Good night, lover."

Her over-the-top delivery helped lessen the stress of the situation. Stifling his own laugh, Quinn said, "I prefer sir or lord and master. You may choose between the two."

"Yeah, that's not going to happen." She turned on her side, facing away from him. "Good night, Quinn."

"Good night, Orlando."

Orlando had been wrong in her assessment. If he'd curled up on the hard floor, he would have had a better night's sleep.

After they said good night, he lay awake for what must have been a couple of hours, her mere presence a magnet, pulling at every inch of him. She was so close. All he would have to do was slide his arm a few centimeters to touch her. But he knew he couldn't allow himself to do that. Contact might eat away at his resistance, until slipping an arm around her would seem like a good idea.

Then pulling her close.

Nuzzling her neck.

Kissing her shoulder.

The sense of her nearness finally grew so great that he had to retreat to the bathroom to prevent himself from shouting in frustration. Once he had calmed down, he returned to bed. This time, he lay above the top sheet so that it could act as a barrier, albeit a thin one, between them. The trick worked, and he was able to finally fall asleep. It did not, however, prevent him from waking several times, needlessly worried he'd unconsciously crawled back under.

By the time his alarm went off, stirring Orlando from her slumber, he was sitting at the table, drinking a second cup of coffee.

She stretched, sat up, and looked at him, her sleep-mussed hair dangling over one eye. "Is that coffee?"

"It's instant."

"Make me two cups, then."

He smiled. "At your service."

Sunday, their first full day in Mexico City, was prep day.

They spent the morning walking the streets around the mission's location, familiarizing themselves with the multiple ways in and out of the area.

"That's the door we're using?" Orlando asked as they walked down the alley behind the building where the event would take place.

"Yeah."

She looked around. "You can't leave a car here."

The alley was narrow, no place for a vehicle to be stowed for any length of time.

"There's a parking garage around the corner. We'll leave it there."

She nodded, and headed over to where several large pipes and a few metal boxes were attached to the outside of the structure. This was where the power entered the building. After studying everything, she looked around and pulled out a set of lockpicks.

"Keep an eye out," she said.

Quinn scanned the alley while she worked on a lock to one of the metal boxes. There were two cameras on the back of the building, but Orlando had created loops of the empty alley on her computer before they headed this way. Anyone watching the feeds would think all was quiet.

Quinn heard a click and a *thunk* as the box door swung open. After a few moments, he glanced over his shoulder. "Well?"

"It's a bit of a rat's nest but should be easy enough. When the time comes, it shouldn't take me more than ten minutes to set things up."

She shut the case, and they continued walking to the end of the alley. There, Orlando pulled her laptop from her backpack and switched the cameras back to a live view.

After a quick lunch of street tacos and *aguas frescas de horchata*, they took a taxi to an auto service garage several kilometers east of the mission site.

Even though this was Sunday, the sounds of work echoed from inside the building. Quinn and Orlando entered the main garage area, and walked over to where a young mechanic had his head under the hood of a Chevy Tornado truck.

After a few moments, the guy looked over and said in Spanish, "Can I help you?"

"We're looking for Denis Aguilar," Quinn responded in kind. "Is he around?"

The man twisted around and looked toward the other cars being worked on. "Denis! Customer!"

A man ducked out from under a Volkswagen Clasico that was jacked in the air on a hydraulic lift two bays away. Bald with a bushy black moustache, he appeared to be north of thirty-five. He reminded Quinn of a Latin version of Peter, with just a bit more height.

Upon seeing Quinn and Orlando, Aguilar pulled a rag off the top of a rolling tool table, wiped his hands, and walked over.

"What can I do for you?" the man said, a hint of irritation at the edge of his helpful expression.

"Roberto Ortiz sent us," Quinn said.

The man's annoyance vanished upon hearing the recognition code. "Roberto, yes. I talked to him this morning. Said you needed to borrow a truck for a day or two?"

"That's correct."

"This way. Please."

Aguilar led them into the front office, where he removed a set of keys from a desk, and then escorted Quinn and Orlando out a side door into the lot surrounding the shop.

"It's right back here," he said.

A blue Nissan Frontier pickup truck sat directly behind the building. The model put it at about four years old, and while it showed some wear, no one would ever call it rundown. Just the kind of vehicle that would blend into the city. And, as requested, the bed was covered by a hard plastic lid.

Aguilar opened the passenger door. "As you can see, it is nice and clean," he said, acting like they were normal customers borrowing the truck.

"Looks perfect," Quinn said. The condition of the interior was consistent with the vehicle's age. "Can we see the back?"

"Of course."

Aguilar led them around to the bed and used one of the keys to open the cover. A black, easy-to-clean plastic liner protected the bed itself. At the end next to the cab sat a metal storage box that stretched from side to side, and appeared to be bolted in place.

"It's empty at the moment, but you can put your tools in there," Aguilar said, following Quinn's gaze. He picked another key on the ring and held it up. "This will open it."

"Thank you," Quinn said. "This will work fine."

Aguilar handed the keyring over. "Anything else I can help you with?"

"No. I think this is it."

"Please bring it back with a full tank of gas. And try not to scratch it up."

Aguilar gave them a smile and headed back around the side of the building. After Quinn and Orlando heard the garage door open and close, Orlando moved over to the corner and peered around it.

"He's gone," she whispered.

Quinn hopped into the bed, and used the key the man had shown him to unlock the toolbox. Unlike Aguilar's description, the box was most definitely not empty. Inside he found a brief-case-sized container holding two pistols—a SIG SAUER P226 for Quinn and a Glock 17 for Orlando—four sound suppressors, three spare magazines each, two boxes of 9mm ammunition, and one of the special bullets Quinn had requested. In a duffel bag beside the case were two sets of janitorial coveralls, a box of rubber gloves, and a box of disposable surgical hats.

"We're good," he said as he relocked the box.

They headed out, Orlando playing navigator and guiding them to the first of a handful of hardware stores, where they began picking up the items they had not requested from Aguilar. Four stores later, they had everything they needed, and headed to the abandoned construction site where they would perform their final task for the day.

Quinn had picked out the location before leaving Los Angeles, after his research confirmed the site had not only been sitting untouched for over two years, but more importantly, it was also tied up in the courts and not likely to see a resumption of construction for several more years.

The horrendous Mexico City traffic meant they didn't reach the site until nearly 7:30 p.m. That was fine. What they had to do was better done in the dark.

Quinn parked the truck near a partially built structure at the center of the property. He and Orlando then grabbed the shovels they had purchased and made their way to a pile of dirt, halfway to the back property line. At the base of the pile they dug a hole, approximately six feet long by three feet wide, and five feet deep.

"That should do it," Quinn said, as he tossed the last shovelful of dirt onto the existing mound.

After Orlando helped him out of the ditch, they hid their shovels inside the unfinished building and headed back to town.

"So, where are you taking me to dinner?" Orlando asked.

"Oh, I'm taking *you* to dinner?"

"Of course you are. Someplace nice, I think. After that, maybe someplace with music."

"Hey, Ms. I Need a Decent Night of Sleep. Tomorrow is show-time. Don't you think it would be better to pick up something to eat and head to the apartment so we could turn in early?"

"Oh, please. We're going to have plenty of rest time before the action starts. And come on, I haven't been out in *ages*." She looked at him, puppy dog eyes on full display. "Please. I promise to get you home before your mom sends the police out looking for you."

He chuckled. "Fine. But you need to pick out the place. Unless you want to drive."

She looked out at the sea of brake lights and pulled out her phone. "Let me see what I can dig up."

It was a night to be remembered.

For Quinn, there was really no other way to describe it.

To start, dinner was wonderful, and not just the food and the view of the city's historical center. It was the conversation and the laughs and the memories Quinn would remember most.

Not once did either of them bring up Durrie. Instead they stuck to recounting missions that hadn't involved him, and told each other stories from their lives before they joined the world of espionage.

It was like he was sitting across from the old Orlando again. The one who had not yet become romantically involved with Durrie. The fun Orlando. The teasing Orlando. The best friend Quinn had ever had Orlando.

After dinner they found a club a few blocks away, where they enjoyed some Mexican rock and roll, and where Orlando, after they both had a few more drinks, convinced Quinn to get up and dance with her. As much as he enjoyed it, he almost wished he'd said no. Seeing her moving around like that, right in front of him, reminded him of the torture he'd gone through the night before, a torture he knew would be repeated when they returned to the apartment.

As they sat back down, he casually glanced at his watch and shot to his feet again. It was a quarter after midnight. They needed to be awake again in less than four hours. "We've got to go."

"Relax, it's early."

"Um, no. It's not."

He held out his wrist so she could see the time.

"That can't be right," she said.

"Check."

She pulled out her phone. "Crap."

Quinn paid the bill and they caught a taxi back to their apartment.

As they lay on the bed, Orlando under the sheet, Quinn on top, Orlando said, "Thank you for tonight."

"Don't thank me. I'm going to make Peter pay for everything."

"I mean…for helping me forget for a little while."

He lay there, unmoving, not sure what to say. She'd given him an opening to talk about Durrie. He wanted to step through it, to find out exactly what had been going on so he could figure out how to help her. But if he took the opportunity, he'd be doing exactly the opposite of what she was thanking him for. After a few seconds, he said only, "I had a fun night, too. Thanks."

She smiled and turned away from him. "You set the alarm?"

"I did."

"Good night, sweetheart."

"Good night, sugar bear."

9

Quinn groaned as he peeled his eyelids open and reached for his phone to turn off the alarm. The time on the screen read 3:55 a.m.

"Already?" Orlando croaked beside him.

"I blame you."

He climbed out of bed and retreated to the bathroom, where he used a wash towel to give himself a quick standing bath, then threw his clothes on. When he came out, Orlando was leaning against the wall next to the door, her eyes half closed.

"I made you coffee," she said with a nod toward a cup on the table.

He barely tasted the liquid as it went down, but the only thing that really mattered was the caffeine boost he hoped to get from it.

When Orlando was ready, they grabbed their bags and headed out.

The parking garage around the corner from the job site was a small setup—two stories with additional parking on the roof, about thirty spots per level. Quinn would have preferred something a bit larger, more anonymous, but this one was most convenient. Plus, unlike other places, it was open twenty-four hours.

The attendant sitting on a chair by the gate rose as Quinn pulled up.

"I understand you allow long-term stays," Quinn said.

"Depends on what you mean by long term," the man said.

"Three days at the most." In truth, it would be closer to twenty hours than seventy-two.

The man told him the price, and Quinn paid.

"You go over that time, it'll be extra," the man said as he moved to the gate controls.

"No problem."

The man pushed a button and the arm rose.

Most of the spaces on the ground floor were already taken. That was fine. Quinn wanted someplace out of the attendant's sight, and found the perfect spot on the second floor, next to one of the stairwells.

While Orlando got to work on her laptop, Quinn climbed into the truck bed, and added the weapons and other items Aguilar had supplied them to the duffel containing their other supplies. When he was finished, he locked up the bed and stuck his head into the cab.

"How we looking?" he asked.

"Just a couple seconds." She tapped away for a bit longer, and then said, "All set." She closed the screen and stuffed the computer into her backpack. The cameras behind the job site were now once again looping footage showing a deserted area.

"Here," he said as they walked to the stairs, handing her a pair of rubber gloves.

They pulled them on, and took the stairs down to an exit that let out onto the street. After making sure no one was around, they made their way to the alley.

During their daylight scout, Quinn had noted the lack of rear lighting fixtures on the buildings lining the passageway. Now that it was dark, even fewer of them seemed to be working, and those that were on did little to cut through the inky darkness. Down the alley they went, unseen in the shadows.

First stop was the electrical box Orlando had examined the previous day. Quinn stood behind her, shielding the rest of the alley from the penlight she used. After opening the box, Orlando identified the power sources to each floor, attached clamp-like devices around them, and then pulled a cell phone out of her bag and turned it on. It was a cheap flip phone she had modified with extra ports on the side, into which she plugged the wires hanging off the back of the clamps. She carefully situated the phone inside the box and closed the door.

When activated via a call, the phone would trigger whichever clamp she had designated—or all of them—to cut off the power running through the wire attached to that clamp. This was merely a safety precaution, in case things didn't go well and they needed the distraction of a power outage.

To prevent the very remote chance of someone opening the box and discovering the phone and clamps, Orlando removed a thin strand of sticky cord from her bag, and ran it along the edge of the box's door where it touched the housing.

She next pulled out a book of matches. "Clear?"

Quinn looked both ways down the alley. "Clear."

She lit the match and touched the flame to the cord. The moment the substance flared to life, she stepped back and turned away. White light illuminated their small portion of the alley as if it were daylight. This might have been a problem if it had lasted long, but the substance was designed to burn hot and fast and, just as importantly, quiet.

Within five seconds darkness descended once more.

Orlando flicked on her penlight as she and Quinn turned to the box. The cord was gone. In its place were burn scars where the intense heat had welded the electric box's door closed.

Orlando removed a large bottle of water from her bag and poured it down the front of the box, speeding up the cooling process. When the bottle was empty, she used a rag to dry the surface.

"Still too hot?" Quinn asked.

She shook her head. "It should be okay."

From the duffel, Quinn removed a paintbrush and the small can of paint they'd purchased. "You want to do it?"

"Be my guest," she said.

Quinn opened the can and proceeded to paint over the scorch marks. It wouldn't fool anyone who got close enough, but from a couple of meters away, most people wouldn't notice anything wrong.

The closed can and the brush went into a Ziploc bag, which was then stowed in the duffel for disposal later.

Intel had provided information on the building's alarm system, allowing Orlando to isolate the back door and disconnect it from the system the previous morning, while making the software think everything was fine. At least, that's what she had done in theory. They were about to test whether or not she had been successful.

Quinn picked the deadbolt first, and disengaged the lock in the handle. Slowly, he eased the door away from the frame.

No flashing lights. No ringing bells.

He gave Orlando an appreciative nod and she stared back, clearly questioning his intelligence for having doubted her.

They moved across the threshold into a dimly lit corridor, where only every third overhead was on. From the building's blueprints, Quinn knew the door at the far end of the hall opened onto the main lobby, where the building's sole nighttime security guard was stationed. Three of the structure's four elevators were also accessed there. Only the freight elevator was in the back half of the building, its entrance four meters down the corridor's back door.

When it was time for the termination, this elevator would take them up to the job site, though not in the way most would travel. But that was still many hours away.

They made their first trip to Felix Ruiz's office via the back stairs. At the landing for each floor, they paused at the door for a quick listen. As they'd hoped, the building was dead quiet. Any early-bird employees weren't likely to show up for another hour at least.

Upon reaching floor five, they waited an entire minute before easing out of the stairwell, into a room approximately five meters square. Two large plastic bins sat in one corner, each marked BASURA—trash—and in another lived a metal cabinet, with nothing denoting its use. The only other exit was a set of double doors on the wall to the right.

They approached the doors and listened again. Satisfied no one was on the other side, Quinn started to pull it open, but stopped when one of the hinges squeaked.

Orlando reached into the duffel bag hanging from his shoulder and pulled out a can of WD40. She squirted the hinges on both sides of the exit, then wiped away the excess liquid with one of the paper towels.

Quinn gently pushed the door again. This time it opened without a sound.

They walked down the corridor to Ruiz's suite.

The attorney had the good sense to have his own alarm system. Unfortunately for him, the company that had installed it kept records on a computer connected to the internet. Which meant that not only did Quinn and Orlando know the make and model of the system, they also knew exactly where the door contacts were and where each motion sensor had been placed.

Oh, and they'd also obtained the alarm company's override deactivation code.

Quinn picked the locks, then looked at Orlando, who gave him a nod.

He opened the door and she moved quickly into the room, to the sound of a low *beep-beep-beep* coming from the control box on the wall behind the receptionist's desk. As soon as she keyed in the code, the beeping stopped, and a green light appeared above the keypad.

To the right of the box was a doorless entry to a hallway running right and left, with four doors leading off it. One was to a conference room, another to a storage closet, and the final two to offices.

Ruiz's office was the larger of the latter, and, in addition to a desk, included a seating area with an armchair and a couch. The latter of which, on closer inspection, could be turned into a bed.

"Please tell me he doesn't use that for what I think he does," Orlando said when Quinn lifted a cushion to show her.

"Well, he *does* have a reputation."

"If you're trying to make me throw up, you're doing a pretty good job."

He pushed the cushion back in place. "I'll take the desk. You take the cabinets."

Before Quinn touched anything, he took a picture of the desk so that he could put everything back in the same place when he finished. The desktop itself held nothing of real value—a couple of files in an out tray, some correspondence to be opened, a multi-line phone, and a wooden box containing a few pens, some paper-clips, and a crucifix. Draped over the desk were power and internet lines for a computer but no actual machine. That jibed with the mission brief that stated Ruiz always carried a laptop.

As Quinn opened each drawer, he again took a picture before going through it. But what he was looking for was not in one of the drawers. It was in a metal clip attached to the underside of the desktop.

He freed the gun and held it up. A Smith & Wesson Colt .45. Assuming its purpose was for Ruiz to protect himself in this very room, it was a lot of firepower for the space.

Quinn pulled out a box from his duffel and set it on the desk beside the gun. Inside were eight rows of six bullets each. Four different calibers, two rows per set.

Quinn popped the magazine out of Ruiz's gun, removed the bullets and the one in the chamber. He replaced them with .45-caliber ammunition from the box, sticking a final new bullet in the chamber.

The ammunition looked identical to that he had taken out, but had two important differences. None of the new bullets contained any gunpowder, nor would their primers work. There was no way for Ruiz to know that without pulling the trigger, however, so if he happened to inspect his weapon, he wouldn't see anything wrong.

Quinn put the live bullets into the empty holes in his case, reseated the gun in its clip, and returned the case to his duffel.

"Find anything interesting?" he asked.

"Not really," Orlando said. "I'm guessing all the good stuff's on his computer."

"Let's finish up. I don't know about you but I could use a nap. I mentioned before that I blame you for the lack of sleep, didn't I?"

Orlando removed her backpack and set it on the armchair. "You did, but you were wrong. It was your fault."

"Mine? I wasn't the one who wanted to go out last night."

"But you *were* the one who was supposed to be keeping track of time." She pulled two cameras out of her bag and tossed one to Quinn.

As he caught it, he said, "I don't believe we ever established that."

"We didn't have to. It was presumed."

"*I* never presumed it."

"But I did. Which means it was your fault." She placed her camera in a bookcase directly across from Ruiz's desk. "How's this look?"

Quinn studied it for a moment. "What happens if he needs one of those books on that shelf?"

"If he does, it'll be the first time in months. Whoever does the dusting in this place hasn't hit this area in a while."

Quinn found a spot for his camera on the window frame, half hidden by the blinds. After Orlando gave him the thumbs-up, they exited the office and put cameras in the conference room, other office, and lobby before leaving the suite.

They headed back toward the stairwell and were about

halfway down the hallway when they heard one of the elevators whir to life. They picked up their pace. The elevator turned out to be one of the three main ones, and it stopped before reaching the fifth floor.

In the maintenance room, Quinn pried open the service elevator doors far enough for Orlando to lean into the shaft.

"It's on the ground floor," she confirmed.

They proceeded down the stairs and stopped on the second floor. Once more, Quinn forced open the elevator doors, this time all the way. Using the shaft's support railings, Orlando climbed down onto the top of the elevator. While she did this, Quinn retrieved a rope from his duffel and tied one end to the bag's handgrips. Once Orlando was settled on the elevator, he lowered the bag to her, and then swung into the shaft himself.

Getting the doors closed again from the inside was tricky, but after a few moments he was able to get them shut. He climbed down and joined Orlando.

The top of an elevator wasn't the most comfortable place to spend a day, but at least there was enough room for one of them at a time to lie down and sleep.

"You go first," he whispered.

"You look more tired than me. You should go."

"My gig, my call. You sleep first."

She shrugged. "All right. I'm not going to argue with you."

She lay down.

"Try not to snore," he said.

"I never snore."

He laughed under his breath.

"What?"

"Nothing."

"I never snore."

"Okay, sure. But if I give you a kick don't take it personally. It just means be quiet."

"Ha. Ha," she said. Then, after a beat, "Don't kick too hard."

10

The first time the service elevator moved was at 9:36 a.m.

Quinn, still on guard duty, jerked in surprise. His sleep-deprived mind had been drifting and he hadn't heard anyone enter the car below. Orlando, on the other hand, didn't even budge.

It moved twice more before Quinn's turn to sleep, and according to Orlando, had taken an additional seven trips by the time he woke just after six p.m.

At seven p.m., the car headed up again. While in transit, the person inside rapped against the side three times, then two, then three again.

Timo Hokkanen, the mission's assassin, had arrived.

As soon as Hokkanen exited on the fifth floor and the doors closed, Orlando opened her computer, and brought up the feeds from the cameras she and Quinn had installed throughout Ruiz's suite. She plugged in an audio splitter, which was attached to two sets of earbuds. She gave one set to Quinn and donned the other.

Ruiz was the only one in his suite and was sitting behind his desk. His secretary, who also served as receptionist and often stayed late, had received a phone call from her son's school around five p.m., informing her that her son had been caught sneaking into a classroom and she needed to pick him up right away. The call had not come from the school, of course, but from one of Peter's operatives.

A muffled knock caused Ruiz to look up from his laptop. He started to call out, but then seemed to remember he was alone. As he rose, he reached under his desk and pulled out the gun. After slipping it into his waistband at the small of his back, and draping his suit jacket over it, he proceeded through the offices to the front door and opened it to find the Finnish assassin outside.

"*Señor* Bale?" Ruiz said.

"*Sí,*" Hokkanen replied.

The seven-p.m. meeting between Ruiz and a potential client named Robert Bale had also been set up by Peter's people.

Stepping out of the way, Ruiz said, "Come in."

At 195 centimeters tall, Hokkanen could barely pass through the doorway without ducking. As far as Quinn knew, the man was the tallest assassin in the business. And it was this height that made him particularly good at a very specific method of killing.

After Hokkanen was inside and the door closed, Ruiz said, "This way," and turned his back on the man who he thought was a new client, intending to lead him to the back office.

The lawyer had taken only one step, however, before Hokkanen reached over the man's head and yanked a garrote around Ruiz's neck. The assassin's hands were large enough that he needed only one to twist both ends of the garrote so that it squeezed tight against the target's skin. With his free hand, Hokkanen pulled Ruiz to his chest and manhandled him to the floor. There, the assassin wrapped a leg around Ruiz's lower body, effectively cutting off all resistance as he continued to strangle the attorney.

Ruiz shot his hands up to the garrote to pull it away, but when that proved impossible, he reached around for his gun. Unfortunately for him, Hokkanen had him pinned so that it was impossible for him to reach it. Terror grew on Ruiz's face.

What was missing from his expression, however, was surprise.

Being in bed with a cartel came with some very sweet rewards, but also with risks few people would accept. Ruiz had been one of the few, and those risks were now a reality.

It didn't take much longer for the life to fade from his eyes. Hokkanen, however, maintained his deathly embrace for another full minute before releasing the lawyer's husk. Being a professional in this business meant not leaving things to chance.

That was Quinn's cue. He slipped through the escape hatch on top of the car, made sure Hokkanen had turned the elevator off, and exited onto the fifth floor. When he reached the door to Ruiz's suite, he rapped on it twice, then twice again.

Hokkanen let him in and shut the door.

"Nice work," Quinn said.

The assassin grinned. "You were watching, yes?"

"I was."

"I prefer targets to have a little more fight in them," Hokkanen said. "But I'll take this. Easy money, am I right?"

Quinn glanced at the man's bare hands. To prevent tipping off Ruiz, Hokkanen had not worn gloves. "Touch anything?" Quinn asked.

He had not seen the assassin do so, but there'd been a time gap between when Quinn left the elevator and when Hokkanen let him into the office.

"Just the door handle," the man said.

"What about the garrote? Where is it?"

Hokkanen tapped the pocket of his suit coat. "I have it."

Quinn pulled out a large Ziploc bag from his pocket and held it open. "Hand it over."

The cord would be covered in Ruiz's DNA, making it a piece of evidence that needed to be destroyed.

"It's only been used the once. It still has a lot of life in it."

"You know that's not the way this works," Quinn said.

Quinn was well aware Hokkanen—who had more time in the business—was testing him. It wasn't the first time a veteran agent had pulled something similar.

The standoff lasted another couple of seconds, before Hokkanen laughed and retrieved the garrote.

After he dumped it in the bag, Quinn said, "You put the weapon in your pocket. I'm going to need the jacket, too."

With a frown, Hokkanen pulled off the coat and handed it to Quinn. "I'd appreciate it if you didn't mention the jacket to Peter. I'd like to report it as damaged and bill him."

"I don't know anything about a jacket," Quinn said.

"Thank you."

It was a small favor, one that would increase Hokkanen's trust in Quinn, and make easier any work they did together in the future.

Quinn pulled a pair of disposable rubber gloves out of his bag. "Use these on your way out."

Hokkanen pulled them on. "Until next time."

The assassin opened the door and disappeared into the hallway. To avoid being seen by anyone below, he would take the stairs to the roof, and then hop two buildings over before descending to the street. Before the night was over, he'd be on a plane out of the country.

Quinn pulled a rolled-up body bag out of the duffel and laid it on the floor next to Ruiz. As he moved the flaps to the side, two raps echoed off the door, and then one. He opened it and let Orlando in. Now that Hokkanen was gone, they wouldn't have to worry about him seeing Orlando and potentially mentioning the fact to Peter.

They lifted Ruiz into the bag but left it unzipped.

Quinn reentered the public hallway and walked its entire length. While only one other suite on the fifth floor was currently leased, he still paused at each entrance and listened. Every one of them was dead quiet. He continued to the public elevators and confirmed the cars were sitting at the ground floor. Finally, he checked the back room where the service elevator and rear stairs were located. No one there, nor were there any sounds of steps in the stairwell.

He reentered Ruiz's office and found Orlando vacuuming the carpet with their handheld vac, around where Hokkanen had taken down Ruiz.

"We're clear," he said. He grabbed the special ammo box out of the duffel, pulled the Colt from behind Ruiz's back, and headed through the suite to Ruiz's personal office.

Sitting on the desk was Ruiz's laptop computer and a pad of paper with notes written on the top sheet. Quinn set the ammo box on the desk. Turned out the dummies were unnecessary, but in Quinn's world that was a sign of a job well done.

He removed the faux ammo, returned the original bullets to the weapon, and snapped the pistol back into the brackets under the desk. He pushed Ruiz's chair under the desk like how it had been when they did their walk-through, and turned off the desk lamp. After closing the computer, he picked it up along with the pad of paper, then exited the room, flipping off the overhead light on his way out.

Now it would look like Ruiz had left for the evening. And when someone eventually started looking for him, all indications would be that whatever had happened to the attorney, it hadn't occurred here.

As Quinn reentered the suite's lobby, Orlando was placing the vacuum's dust bag in the body bag with Ruiz.

"Doorknob?" he asked.

"Not yet."

He placed the items from Ruiz's office in the duffel bag before pulling out a small bottle of bleach spray and a rag. These he used to thoroughly wipe down the doorknob and the area around it.

After a spray of odor neutralizer to eliminate the heavy bleach scent, he turned back to the room and looked around. "Everything looks good. You see anything?"

Orlando scanned the space and shook her head. "I think that's it."

"Zip him up."

The most difficult item on their agenda was lifting Ruiz through the elevator access hatch and onto the roof of the car. Quinn pulled from up top while Orlando pushed from below, both straining with the awkward load. But centimeter by centimeter the body bag cleared the opening, until it finally rested on the surface beside Quinn.

Orlando turned the elevator back on and pushed the button for the first floor. As the car descended, Quinn pulled Orlando up through the roof opening. Before they'd even reached the fourth floor, the hatch was closed again.

When the elevator stopped on the ground floor, the doors opened automatically, stayed that way for twenty seconds, and closed again.

It wasn't long before Quinn and Orlando heard the muffled clicks of shoes on tiled floor. As expected, the after-hours movement of the elevator had drawn the attention of the guard.

A few moments later, the elevator doors opened again.

A step inside, and a step back out, followed by the doors shutting.

The clicking of shoes again, this time moving toward the back of the building. Though the noise was faint, Quinn was sure he heard the rear entrance door opening.

For several moments all was silent, then the clicks made a third appearance, this time moving from the back of the building, past the elevator, and toward the front lobby, where they soon faded to nothing.

Quinn and Orlando waited thirty minutes, in case the guard decided to take a second look around. When he failed to show up, Orlando pulled out her computer and performed her magic trick with the cameras covering the back of the building. Quinn then slipped into the elevator car, pried the doors apart just wide enough for him to pass through, and entered the hallway.

From there it was a short trip out the rear door and back to the parking garage. A different guy was working the entrance as Quinn pulled out. A flash of the prepaid ticket resulted in the gate swinging open, with barely a glance from the attendant.

Quinn drove the long way around and entered the alley from the opposite end, to avoid anyone near the parking garage noticing his actions. After parking behind Ruiz's building, he unlocked the bed cover, raised it a good meter, and reentered the structure.

Back in the elevator, he tapped twice on the wall to let Orlando know it was him. She opened the hatch, handed down the duffel and her backpack, and then they switched places.

Quinn lowered the body bag through the hole feet first and leaned down with it until it touched the floor. Though Orlando was only about three quarters the size of the dead lawyer, she was in prime shape. When Quinn was sure she had control of the body, he let go and lowered himself beside her.

Together they set the body on the floor.

Orlando rolled her neck to the side, stretching it.

"You okay?" Quinn whispered.

"Yeah, just—"

Click. Click. Click.

Without another word, they moved to the front of the elevator, taking position at either side of the door.

As the guard—or whoever it was—neared the front of the car, Quinn tensed. But the steps continued for another couple of meters. A door opened. From where the sound came from, it could only be the door to the stairwell. This was confirmed when the click of the shoes traveled into the well and began moving upward.

"Must be on his rounds," Orlando whispered.

Quinn concentrated on the steps. When it sounded like they had reached the second-floor landing, he said, "Come on."

He draped the duffel's straps over his shoulders and pried the doors open again. They picked up the body bag, exited the elevator, and headed down the hallway and out the rear exit.

With a single swing to gain momentum, they hefted Ruiz into the back of the truck and tossed the duffel bag in beside him. Quinn shut the cover and twisted the latch into place but didn't waste time locking it.

He raced around and jumped into the driver's seat. Orlando was already buckled in on the passenger's side, her computer out and opened. He pulled away, his gaze flicking back and forth between the alley and his rearview mirror. By the time Ruiz's building disappeared from sight, the door at the back had not moved.

"Loops are off," Orlando said. She typed again, this time pecking the keyboard for over fifteen seconds. "Emergency distraction disabled."

This meant she had sent a message to the phone in the power box, triggering it to self-destruct. By the time someone thought to pry the box open, the phone and the wires attaching it to the clamps would be a hardened glop of plastic at the bottom.

Quinn was starting to relax when a thought hit him. He slammed on the brakes. "The hatch."

"What do you—" She closed her eyes, also remembering. "Oh, crap."

In their desire to avoid the guard, they had left the hatch in the service elevator open. If Quinn had done that in his apprentice days, Durrie would have laid into him for weeks. A similar reprimand now would be no less deserved.

Every obsessive-compulsive fiber in his body was telling him to turn around and fix the problem, but the survival side of his brain countered with *It's not worth the risk.*

He heard the passenger door open and looked over as Orlando hopped to the ground.

"I'll be right back," she said, and disappeared before he could reply.

He pulled to the side of the road and almost jumped out of the car to race after her. But while seeing a woman running down the road might be odd, seeing a man apparently chasing her would be downright memorable.

There was nothing he could do but wait.

He kept his eyes focused on the rearview mirror as the minutes ticked off. Four, five, then six. At the start of the seventh minute, a small silhouette appeared in the distance, not running, walking. Though it looked like Orlando, it wasn't until the shadowy form was a few car lengths away that he knew for sure.

When she opened the door and climbed in, he said, "What the hell were you thinking?"

"I was thinking we needed to be thorough."

"I'm the one in charge, remember? I make these decisions." He looked out the front window and took a moment to calm down. "Did you get it shut?"

"Of course."

"How?"

She was much too short to reach the hatch on her own.

"Mop handle."

He looked at her again, his eyes wide.

She shrugged. "Improvise, right?"

He held his stare for a moment longer and then laughed. After a second, Orlando joined in.

When Quinn finally caught his breath, he said, "Next time, can we at least talk about it for a second before you run off?"

"That'll depend on the situation, won't it?"

He snorted and shook his head, then started the engine and pulled away.

They unzipped the body bag and upended it, so that Ruiz and the trash from the scene tumbled into the hole they had dug the night before. After the body was stretched out, Quinn poured two gallons of a chemical cocktail over the body, mixed from ingredients he and Orlando had picked up on their tour of hardware stores. It wasn't the best solution he had ever used, but it was pretty good given what was available to them.

In seventy-two hours, the body would be unrecognizable. At the end of a week, even the best forensic technicians would have a hard time pulling any useful information from the remains.

Quinn and Orlando refilled the hole. After this, they repeatedly jabbed their shovels into the pile of dirt beside the grave, creating a miniature landslide that cascaded over the spot, concealing it from sight. At worst, it would be at least a year before any of the dirt was moved again. In the best-case scenario, the construction at the site would be put off for a decade or maybe forever.

Quinn and Orlando caught an early morning flight to Dallas, from where they would take separate flights back to California—Quinn on a nonstop to Los Angeles, and Orlando making a plane change in Phoenix before continuing to San Diego.

"Thank you," Orlando said before they left for their separate gates. "I can't tell you how much this means to me."

Quinn smiled, but she could tell something was troubling him.

"You aren't going to say anything to Peter, right?" she asked.

"No. Of course not. It's just…"

"Just what?"

"I'm supposed to also supervise him on whatever the next mission Peter puts him on. What happens if Durrie backs out of that one, too?"

"He won't. I promise."

Quinn almost said something, but held it back. This time she didn't prod him, as she was pretty sure he would remind her she'd promised Durrie would be on this job, too.

"If for some reason he doesn't show up," she said, "I won't try to talk you out of reporting it." She meant it, though she was determined to not let things get to that point.

She slept most of the way to San Diego, then watched the city rise up around her as her plane descended toward the airfield.

Durrie wasn't home when she arrived at the house. She had texted him from Dallas so he should have been here waiting for her. Normally, when she had work and he didn't, he'd be home when she returned.

She called him, but after five rings the call went to voice mail. After the beep, she said, "I'm home. I was thinking maybe we could grab some dinner. Let me know if you're up for it."

She texted him a similar message, but received no response.

Her two days in Mexico had made her all but forget how stressful her life was. The oppressiveness now came crashing back with a vengeance. She felt the weight of a thousand worries pressing down on her, trying to shove her through the floor and into the earth itself. And as if that wasn't enough, the dull headache that had been her constant companion these past few months began throbbing again.

She took a shower, hoping that would ease some of the pain, but within minutes her hands were pressed against the wall, water pouring over her, as she was overwhelmed by the inability to come up with even one idea for how to pull Durrie out of his funk.

He had never been an easy man to love.

His gruff, sarcastic demeanor had rubbed more than a few people the wrong way. But he'd always been a total professional who respected those good at their jobs. A respect that had extended to her, even when she'd been a newly minted apprentice with Durrie's sometime partner, Abraham Delger.

She hadn't planned on falling in love with Durrie. Nor had she realized he had any romantic interest in her. Not until the day he'd asked her on a date. She'd said yes more out of shock than anything else.

He'd been the perfect gentleman. Kind and generous and interested in her. And funny, too. She had laughed so much that night that she'd found herself saying yes to a second date without hesitation. It didn't matter that he was considerably older than her. She enjoyed being around him. Over the coming weeks and months, she fell more and more into his orbit, until one day she woke up and realized she loved him.

It was surprising, really.

If you had asked her a few years ago who in her professional circle she might end up with, she would have guessed Quinn. They had a ton in common and clearly enjoyed each other's company, so she would have welcomed a relationship with him. But he had never done anything to indicate he would have been open to one with her, too.

He was always so respectful toward everyone, but toward her especially. Sometimes to the point of madness. If the average person clocked in at around five or six on a respectful scale, Durrie would have hit around seven point five. But Quinn? Quinn would easily land somewhere off the scale. Say, at fifteen or maybe even twenty.

Not that the possibility of becoming involved with him mattered anymore. For better or worse, she was with Durrie. And she would help him, even if he didn't ask for it.

She went to bed at midnight, having left him several more messages, voice and text. When she opened her eyes again, the room was still dark, and the other side of the mattress still unoccupied. But she sensed something in the room.

She sat up.

"Hello, baby."

Durrie sat in the chair by the door, his hands clasped in his lap.

She reached for the lamp on her nightstand.

"Don't," he said.

She stopped. "Where have you been?"

"Out."

"That's not an answer."

He chuckled and leaned forward, forearms on thighs. "Let's see. I was at the Tin Star for a while. Then Ella Wayne's and Rhythm Bay." He paused. "Oh, yeah. I hit Margo's somewhere in there. Don't ask me to give you the order."

Bars, all of them.

"How much did you have to drink?"

"Not a drop."

She reached over and turned the light on before he could stop her again.

His eyes were clear, and there were none of the usual signs he displayed when inebriated.

"I tried calling you," she said.

"I got your messages."

"Then why didn't you come home?"

"I considered it. But I had too much on my mind."

"Like what?"

He leaned back again. "Oh, I don't know. Maybe like you and Johnny in Mexico City."

She blinked. "What does that mean?"

"Tell me—where did you end up staying?"

"Staying? Um, an apartment."

"That Peter set up."

"Yes."

"A small little place? Studio? One real bed?"

She said nothing.

"I'm right, aren't I?"

"Yes."

He shook his head and let out a quiet snort. "I've stayed there before. Cozy, wasn't it? I bet Quinn really enjoyed it."

"What are you talking about?"

"Come on, baby. I know how much he pines for you. Getting you alone in a place like that must have been like a sign from heaven to him."

She threw back the covers, jumped to her feet, and marched

over to him. "Ignoring for a moment how idiotic you sound, don't you think in a situation like you're suggesting, *I* might have something to say about what would happen?"

A shrug. "I know how you feel about him, too."

"If you believe I would ever cheat on you, you're an even bigger asshole than everyone thinks you are."

She stormed out of the room, almost slapping him on her way out, but stayed her hand as she knew it would do no good.

"Are you saying you *didn't* share the bed with him?" Durrie called after her.

She turned and saw Durrie standing in the doorway now, the grin and knowing look from before tempered by a hint of vulnerability.

"Even if we had, nothing would have happened. Quinn respects you—*and* me—too much to ever do anything that would hurt either of us. You know that."

She could see her words had stung him.

After several seconds, he whispered almost too low for her to hear, "What about you? Would you ever do anything to hurt us?"

Her head ready to explode, she turned away to get her temper under control.

"Everyone makes mistakes," he said.

She whipped back around, a hair's-width from flying down the hall and kicking the living crap out of him. "I'm beginning to think my only mistake was that I let myself fall in love with you." She turned and headed into the living room. "Do *not* follow me. I don't want to see you. I don't want to hear your voice. I don't even want to hear you breathing."

"Orlando…wait."

She kept going.

"I'm…I'm sorry. You're right. I'm being an idiot. I take it all back."

She stormed out of the hallway and over to the breakfast bar that divided the kitchen from the living room, picked up her car keys, and headed for the coat closet.

"Orlando. Please," Durrie said, his voice moving down the hall toward the living room. "I don't know what I was thinking."

A half dozen excellent responses popped into her head, but she suppressed them all. She grabbed her leather jacket and pulled it on over the long T-shirt she'd been sleeping in. She hurried over to the garage door and, as she yanked it open, heard Durrie enter the room behind her.

"Where are you going?" he asked.

Her jaw clenched and her lips sealed, she stepped into the garage and slammed the door closed.

She drove without a destination in mind, her mind reliving not only the horrible conversation she'd just had but all the other moments from the past year or so when Durrie's words and actions had hurt her.

It wasn't until the fog of anger eased that she realized she was heading north, toward Los Angeles. For the next ten minutes, she seriously considered driving all the way to Quinn's house. He was the only one she could talk to about this, and that's what she needed to do right now.

But she only made it as far as Anaheim before admitting to herself that going to him of all people would be a mistake. It would be the quickest way to end her relationship with Durrie. And as painful as that relationship was, she did still love him.

Her paternal grandmother had once said, "It's easy to give yourself to a partner when everything's going well. The true test of a relationship is the ability to do so when things aren't."

She had no idea if he was suffering from an illness or had fully given in to the asshole tendencies he'd always had. Whatever the case, she couldn't turn her back on him.

She took a deep breath, exited just past Disneyland, and reentered the freeway heading south, toward home.

Two days after returning to Los Angeles, Quinn called Orlando, ostensibly to bring her up to speed on how the job closed out, but really because he wanted to say hi and make sure she was okay.

"Peter's happy everything went well," he told her.

"Peter's never happy about anything."

"True enough. How about I say he was pleased."

"That, I'll buy." She paused. "I assume he asked about Durrie."

"He did. I told him everything went well, gave him a rundown of what we did, and told him it all went smoothly."

"That's it?"

"He pressed some, wanted to make sure Durrie hadn't messed anything up, but I stuck to the story."

"So he doesn't suspect anything."

"No, though he did ask if I was still willing to do that next job with Durrie."

"What did you say?"

"I told him of course I was."

Orlando said nothing for a moment, then, "Thank you."

"How's, um, how's Durrie doing?"

"He's fine."

When you know someone, *really* know someone, you pick up on little things, word use or tonal changes, however slight. Things other people wouldn't notice. Things that made you see beyond their words.

When Orlando said, "He's fine," what Quinn heard was "He's still a mess and I don't want to talk about it."

"Will he be ready for the next job?"

"He will. Don't worry."

He didn't even have to try to hear the defensiveness in her tone now. He wished he knew what he could say to help her open up. But he worried that if he pushed even a little, she would shut down. Possibly even pull away from him. That was something he could not risk.

So, instead of providing the lifeline she probably needed, he said, "I'm not worried."

They hung up promising to get together soon in either L.A. or San Diego.

Little did either of them know it would be months before they saw each other again. And when they did, it would be in neither location.

11

The follow-up job Quinn was supposed to do with Durrie was delayed. At first by a week, and then, per Peter, "at least another two." Peter wouldn't divulge the exact reason, only that it had something to do with the target's schedule.

"So, are you saying I have a little free time?" Quinn asked when Peter called him about the latest delay. He was really feeling the need for a little downtime.

Peter snorted over the line. "Right. I've got something coming up in San Francisco that could use your delicate touch, but that's at least a few weeks off. Lucky for you, I have a pair of jobs that are a bit more pressing."

Trying not to sound disappointed, Quinn said, "Great."

Both gigs were in Europe. First up, a simple scene scrubbing in Lisbon. The mission's target had been involved in the theft and sale of military equipment to whoever was willing to pay. Because of the client information he carried in his head, the target could not be eliminated. This was to be an abduction, after which the target would find himself in some out-of-the-way, secret installation, having long conversations with nameless interrogators. Quinn's job was to erase any signs of the kidnapping and plant evidence pointing to the target having left town on a long business trip.

There was a rocky moment near the start of the operation, where the target acted in a way that made the ops leader think he'd been tipped off. But it turned out the man had just been conducting a covert liaison with the wife of a Portuguese cabinet official. They let him have his fun, then as soon as he returned to the hotel room serving as his home, the ops team swung into action. The mission, including Quinn's part, was executed without a hitch.

From there, Quinn traveled to an area south of Amiens, France, where an enforcer for the Italian mob named Jorio had been living for several years under an assumed identity.

But one did not get away with killing two American and three Spanish soldiers indefinitely. Once Jorio was located, those who pulled the strings decided it was time to remove him from the gene pool.

"Eyes on Jorio," the watcher, an operative named Kosar, announced over the comm.

"Copy," Fisher said. He was the ops team's assassin, lying in wait in the trap they had set.

"Copy," Quinn said.

Three ops was the bare minimum on an assignment like this. An additional watcher and an assistant for Quinn, bringing the total to five, would have been more appropriate, but this was a highly sensitive operation.

To say the French were not fans of their allies—or anyone, for that matter—conducting undercover missions on their soil would be an understatement. But bringing them in on the job had not been an option.

A mole controlled by the very mob the target worked for was operating somewhere within French Intelligence. If the French knew what was going on, so would the mob.

The fewer agents involved, the better.

"Turning onto the driveway," Kosar reported.

The dirt driveway was half a kilometer long, running off a country road, along which sat several other farms like this one. The property belonged to a family named Fortier, who sold fresh eggs and milk out of their barn to bolster the income from their crops. Approximately twice a week, the target would drive here to purchase some for himself. Having lived for so many years in the shadows, he knew not to have a set schedule, so there was no specific day or time for his visits.

Kosar had set up cameras on the road in front of Jorio's place, with a view of the man's driveway. Every time the target left his property, the team got into position at the farm. They were able to do this without having to worry about the property's owner because the Fortier family had "won" a ten-day, all-expenses-paid trip to Venice. Early every morning and late every evening, a hired crew came in to deal with the livestock, but the workers were always gone during the range of time when the target would most likely show up.

In the fifty-seven hours since the team had begun its stakeout, Jorio had left his compound five times without coming to the farm. Departure number six was a different story.

"Any traffic?" Fisher asked.

A brief pause while Kosar presumably checked the country road. "All clear."

"Copy."

Quinn waited inside the Fortiers' house, out of the way. Through the living room window, he saw dust billowing up from the target's vehicle as it approached. A few seconds later, he saw the car itself, a purposely ordinary gray sedan.

To sell the illusion nothing unusual was going on, the barn door was open and the Fortiers' sign hung off the side of the building, near the door. It read, in French, SONNEZ LA CLOCHE EN CAS D'ABSENCE—ring the bell if we're not around. Next to this was the end of a rope, leading to a bell mounted high on the wall. The team had even scattered some feed on the ground and let a few of the chickens wander around.

"One hundred meters," Kosar said.

"Copy," Fisher said.

The assassin lay on the farmhouse roof, on the side that sloped away from the barn.

"Fifty meters."

The car slowed as it passed the last of the fields and entered the wide dirt area between the house and the barn. The plan was that after Jorio parked next to the barn and climbed out, Fisher would ease over the apex of the roof and put a bullet through the target's heart as Jorio walked to the bell's rope.

Only instead of parking next to the barn, Jorio stopped halfway across the open space. He sat in his vehicle, engine idling. Quinn could see the man scanning the area.

"I think he's on to us," Quinn said.

"What's going on?" Fisher asked.

Before Quinn could answer, Jorio whipped the car around and raced back toward the driveway.

"He's running!" Kosar said.

Quinn heard scrambling on the roof, followed by three rapid spits from the assassin's suppressed sniper rifle. The bullets punctured the vehicle's rear window, but the car kept moving.

A fourth and fifth spit and the sedan finally veered off course, careening into the field before coming to a stop.

"Dammit," Quinn muttered. His job's difficulty level had just increased.

"Anyone see movement?" Fisher asked.

"I'm repositioning," Kosar replied.

"I don't see anything from here," Quinn said. "Hold on." He grabbed his binoculars and zoomed in on the car. It had stopped at an angle that gave him only a partial view of the front. It took a moment before he was able to make out an arm and shoulder and what he presumed was part of Jorio's head. "He's in the driver's seat. I don't see any movement."

"Kosar," Fisher said. "Anyone other than us see what happened?"

A beat. "There's a truck coming down the main road. No way to know yet if he noticed anything."

"Quinn, I need you to check the target for me. Kosar, keep an eye on that truck."

"Copy," Quinn said.

"Copy," Kosar said.

Quinn drew his weapon and exited the house through the side door. He moved cautiously across the dirt area, his eyes glued to the vehicle. When he reached the rear fender, he paused and looked through the bullet holes in the rear window. Jorio appeared to be draped over the steering wheel, the arm Quinn had seen still in the same position. Either the guy was an excellent actor, or he was indeed out of commission.

Quinn stepped around the side of the sedan, circling out into the wheat that had just missed being crushed by the car. Through the stalks he studied the target, looking for even a hint of movement.

Finally, he approached the driver's-side door. Blood soaked the back of Jorio's shirt. Quinn discerned two entry wounds. The lower shot would have been lethal but death might have taken a while. The upper one, however, had torn through the target's spinal cord within a centimeter or two of his heart. Excellent shooting in both cases, especially given the difficult angle and fleeing subject.

Quinn opened the door, checked the man's pulse, and said into the comm, "He's dead."

Technically that was the moment Fisher's and Kosar's jobs were done. They could have left Quinn alone to take care of the mess without a second thought. But whether it was out of guilt for creating the extra work, or the desire to give a fellow operative a hand, both men pitched in on the cleanup.

There were two big problems. The plan had been for Quinn to drive Jorio's car south to Paris, where—license plates removed and serial numbers filed down—he would leave the vehicle with its keys in the ignition, in an area where it wouldn't likely remain for long. Now, with the damage to the rear window and the bullet holes in the driver's seat, not to mention bloodstains, the repurposing of the vehicle by some random thief was no longer on the table. The car would have to be destroyed in a way that wouldn't cause questions.

The other issue was the grain. In the grand scheme of things, the car hadn't taken out very much at all, the ruined wheat unlikely to put more than the smallest of dents in the Fortiers' income. But since the damage was directly in front of the family's home, there was no way it would go unnoticed. Which would lead the Fortiers to ask questions that may cause problems later.

While Quinn thought about how to handle the situation, he and the other two agents rolled the vehicle out of the field and over the lip between it and the dirt area in front of the barn. They stopped it about a dozen meters from the structure.

Quinn retrieved his gear from inside the house and pulled out a body bag.

"Can you give me a hand with this?" he said to Fisher.

Fisher grabbed one end and they rolled it out.

"I hear you've been working with Durrie again. How's *that* going?"

"Who told you that?"

The assassin shrugged. "Word gets around."

"I heard it, too," Kosar said.

Quinn glanced at both of them, then set his end of the bag on the ground. "It was just one job."

Fisher put his end down. "And?"

"And nothing. Everything went fine." Quinn unzipped the bag and pulled the flap back.

"I know he was your mentor and all, but you should consider yourself lucky. He's gone off the deep end, man. A lot of people I know refuse to work with him."

"Like I said, everything was nice and smooth." Quinn hoped his tone conveyed this was not a conversation he wanted to continue.

The message was received, because Fisher said, "Glad to hear," and neither man brought it up again.

For Quinn, however, the mention of Durrie brought the cover-up back to the forefront of his mind. And that inevitably led to wondering what would happen if Durrie was a no-show for the next job. Or, worse, showed up but did something that jeopardized the mission. Quinn wanted to believe Durrie would perform competently, but in his heart of hearts he didn't think that would happen.

Informing Peter of Durrie's failure would be one of the worst moments in Quinn's life, but if it came to it, he would have no choice.

The more he mulled it over, the more he thought that Durrie missing the mission would be the best solution. Yes, Quinn would still have to tell Peter, but at least the mission would not be compromised and no one would be hurt or, God forbid, killed.

And perhaps getting his mentor blackballed would be a good thing for Durrie, too. It could very well be the kick in the ass the son of a bitch needed to get help.

Orlando would see that, too. She'd have to. She'd understand. Wouldn't she?

Quinn, Fisher, and Kosar put the now full body bag into the sedan's trunk. Quinn sopped up as much of the blood as he could from inside the vehicle, then put the soaked rag into a plastic bag that also went in the trunk.

"There's some plastic sheeting in my bag and some duct tape," he said to Fisher. "Can you get that for me?"

"Sure."

The assassin retrieved the items and helped Quinn wrap the driver's seat in the plastic and secure it with the tape. That would protect Quinn's clothes from getting stained. Unfortunately, he couldn't do anything about the floor around the pedals, and would have to sacrifice one of the two pairs of Nikes he'd brought. Annoying, but sometimes that was the job.

Quinn used a crowbar to knock out the back window. No glass was better than glass with bullet holes in it.

"Any idea what you're going to do about the field?" Fisher asked.

Quinn frowned and looked again at the wheat. "Think we're just going to have to leave it."

"Leave it?"

"Unless you know a way to grow grain to the right height overnight."

"They're going to notice."

"Yeah, they definitely are."

Quinn walked along the car's path and used a rake to obscure tread marks and shoe prints. The dirt in the parking area was harder packed, so the few marks on it weren't enough to be worrisome.

While he couldn't do anything about the damaged grain itself, there was something he could do to temper the Fortiers' response to it.

With his rubber gloves still on, he returned to the house, found a piece of paper in a printer, and wrote a note to the Fortiers, in French, telling them his "son" had lost control of his car and caused the damage. He folded one thousand euros inside the unsigned letter and slipped them into an envelope. He hid the envelope under a planter on the porch. In the next hour or two, he would use a vocal modulator to leave a voice mail on their home phone, letting them know where to find the letter.

"I think that's it, gentlemen," Quinn said. "I appreciate the help."

"What about the rear window?" Kosar said, nodding his chin toward the sedan.

"Not much I can do about that."

"If a cop sees there's no glass, he's going to pull you over."

"I'm not planning on letting a cop see me."

Kosar huffed a laugh, clearly doubting Quinn's ability to pull it off. "You're the expert."

He held out his hand and Quinn shook it.

"You've gotten really good at this," Fisher said, holding out his own hand.

Quinn had worked with him a few times when Quinn first started out on his own, and once or twice back in his apprentice days with Durrie.

He shook the assassin's hand. "Thank you."

With a final goodbye, Fisher and Kosar headed along the back of the field, toward the side road where they'd hidden the car they'd all arrived in.

Quinn called Peter.

"You guys are done?" Peter asked.

"Kosar and Fisher are. My job's been extended a bit."

"Why is that?"

Quinn filled him in.

"You sure there aren't going to be any problems?" Peter asked.

"I'm as sure as I can be."

Peter grunted. "Is there anything you need my help with?"

"As a matter of fact, there is."

Quinn moved the car a couple of kilometers away, down an access road between two more fields of wheat. There he stayed until 2:30 a.m.

The early hour meant not only were there few other travelers on the road, but when there were, he would see their lights long before they neared him. As often as possible, he pulled off the road when this happened, hiding so the other driver wouldn't see the damaged window.

On a side road ten kilometers outside Roubaix, he met up with the vehicle-transportation truck Peter had arranged for him.

He rode up front with the driver, neither saying a word on the entire trip to Rotterdam. You had to love the European Union—no border checks. Just a straight shot out of France through Belgium and into the Netherlands.

Not far from the Rotterdam docks, the truck dropped off Quinn and the sedan at a business that specialized in scrap metal. Waiting for him was an SUV, also courtesy of Peter, parked as requested in a sheltered spot where he would not be observed. He pulled up beside it in the damaged sedan, and transferred his gear and the body bag into the SUV. He then entered the office, looking for the owner.

Over the next ninety minutes, Quinn watched as the fluids were drained from Jorio's sedan, the engine block was ripped off the front, and the car crushed into a metal brick. Before the day was up, the scrap would be loaded onto a cargo ship, bound for a recycling center in Malaysia.

Quinn's next stop was on the other side of the city, at a crematorium he had used before, where the target's body and trash from the clean-up were incinerated. The ashes and few remaining pieces of bone went into a box that he dumped, bit by bit, into different trash bins around town.

By the time he finished, it was after midnight and he was exhausted. But before going to bed, he put in another call to Peter.

After giving him a rundown of the disposal and thanking him for his assistance, Quinn said, "I was thinking, since this other job isn't going to happen for a few weeks at least, I'd love to take a little time off. Maybe hit a beach or something."

"While that's a lovely idea, it's not going to be a few weeks. The job's hot again."

"Seriously?"

"You go on Tuesday."

That was six days away, and with travel back to the States and prep, there wasn't much time left for lounging around on an island.

"All right," Quinn said. "I'll fly back in the morning."

"The information packet will be waiting for you when you get home."

Quinn frowned. "Can't wait."

As promised, Quinn found an email with several attachments sitting in his inbox when he arrived back in Los Angeles midafternoon.

The code name for the job was Operation Redeemer, and the focus of the mission was a Saudi national by the name of Fawar El-Baz, known also as the Falcon. According to the brief, El-Baz had been an early follower of Osama bin Laden, and was rumored to have been involved, at least peripherally, in the planning of the 9/11 attacks. Quietly, the terrorist had begun to form his own splinter operation, which, unlike bin Laden's al-Qaeda, preferred keeping a low profile and letting other groups take credit for its actions. The Falcon had been wreaking havoc throughout Africa and Asia, and was believed to be the mastermind behind a foiled plot to blow up the US, UK, and French embassies in Nigeria two months earlier.

He was a thorn in the side of US Intelligence, who wanted him stopped.

From a source embedded deep within El-Baz's organization, the good folks at the NSA had learned of a trip the terrorist was planning to Rio de Janeiro to meet with Matias Varela, an Argentinian arms dealer, raising new concerns that El-Baz intended to expand his operations into South America.

The terrorist would be arriving via a private jet, with a security detail estimated to be from five to ten men. The mission to intercept him had been previously postponed because El-Baz had rescheduled his trip twice. CIA analysts were now saying there was an eighty-five percent chance the Falcon would make the trip the following Thursday, exactly one week away.

OPERATION REDEEMER

Mission Goal: To capture El-Baz alive and eliminate his men, specific site to be determined.

Your Assignment: Clean the scene and transport the bodies to the airport, where they will be loaded onto El-Baz's jet, which will then be remotely flown over the Atlantic Ocean, where it will crash into the sea, preferably in an area where locating the aircraft will be impossible. All those supposedly on board, including El-Baz, will be presumed dead.

Five to ten bodies were a lot of work for Quinn, even with an on-the-ball Durrie. Thankfully, Peter had authorized him to hire one additional team member.

After going over the brief a second time, Quinn called Durrie. Unsurprisingly, his mentor didn't answer. This gave him an excuse to call Orlando.

"Hi," she answered.

"How's it going?"

"Good. Thanks. How about you?"

"Same." He paused. "So, um, the job is a go."

"*Oh*, that's great," she said, sounding truly excited.

"Yeeaah," he said. "So, um, I tried calling Durrie but he didn't answer. He did get his phone working again, didn't he?"

"Ha! Yeah, he's just…busy."

"So he's not there?"

"Not at the moment."

"Can you tell him to call me? I need to brief him."

"Of course. As soon as I see him."

Quinn hesitated before saying, "I'm going to need him on a plane in four days. Be honest with me. Do you think he'll make it?"

"Of course he will," she said. "That's next Tuesday?"

"Yes."

"Don't worry. He'll be there, and he'll do a great job. I promised, remember?"

"I remember," he said, trying to sound more encouraging than he felt.

"I'll make sure he calls you. And, Quinn, thank you. If it weren't for you, I don't know what I'd do. He really needs this. I can't tell you how much we both appreciate it."

Quinn felt a slight tinge of guilt. Should he tell her the truth? That he was hoping Durrie would drop out? That he thought it would be better for all of them that way?

He couldn't bring himself to do that, so in the end, the only thing he said was, "You're welcome."

12

Orlando wanted to tell Durrie about Quinn's request right away, but he had left right before noon and hadn't returned. She tried calling him but only succeeded in reaching his voice mail, so she sent a text.

When do you think you'll be home?

She thought about mentioning Quinn's need to talk to him but decided against it, fearing doing so would make him stay unreachable all day. Better to wait and tell him in person, and all but force him to make the call in front of her.

She paced the living room, wondering if she should drive out to the Tin Star again. But chances were he was somewhere else, to avoid being found.

She was sure it would be hours before she heard back from him, but twelve minutes after she started carving a path across her floor, her phone dinged with a text.

Six.

That was a little over an hour away.

Now her worry about not being able to get in touch with him turned to concern, about how he would react to the news the mission was on. Other than his agreeing to do it, they had talked little about it. Had he changed his mind? Would he flat out tell her he wasn't interested anymore?

By the time she heard his car pull into the garage at ten after six, she'd worked herself into a ball of nerves. Thank God for the training she'd received from Abraham Delger. Unlike Durrie with Quinn, Abraham had coached her with a patient, understanding hand. Not that he wasn't strict when he needed to be, but he always made sure she understood why he was being hard on her and seemed to really want her to succeed. Durrie, on the other hand, had not been as kind on Quinn.

Early on in her training, Abraham had told her something that had stuck with her. They'd been in Toronto, conducting an information grab on an American businessman suspected of selling banned electronics to a Russian company with close ties to its government. To get into the man's computer, a wireless electronic bug needed to be placed somewhere in the room. Unfortunately, the man had not left his hotel since he arrived, and the growing concern was that the opportunity to extract the data would be missed. Abraham decided Orlando would pose as a hotel maid doing room checks, and use the opportunity to slip the bug under a table.

While Orlando had taken on roles during other operations, those had been in far less dicey situations. This one had her anxious.

"It's okay to be a little scared," Abraham had said. "It means you're taking the situation seriously. But it's also the kind of thing that can get you or others working with you killed. You want to know what I do?"

She nodded.

"Whenever I feel that fear," he said, "I grab on to it, bundle it up, and keep it deep in my gut where others can't see it and where it can't hurt me."

"Easier said than done."

"No, it's not." He smiled. "When you go to his room, don't let your uniform be the only thing that makes him think you're a maid." He pointed at her head. "*Be* the maid in here, and it will show up here." He patted her softly on the cheek. "Become who you are pretending to be, and whoever you're trying to fool will never know the difference."

After they'd successfully finished the mission, he'd enrolled her in nine months of acting lessons in Los Angeles. And while the classes gave her the actual tools she now used whenever she went undercover, it was Abraham's words she always thought of: "Become who you are pretending to be, and whoever you're trying to fool will never know the difference."

Though she still wouldn't admit to herself, a part of her knew she'd been undercover with Durrie for months now, acting understanding when she wanted to scream, uninterested when she knew giving him too much attention might set him off, and unaffected when his actions or inactions made her wonder why she was sticking around.

So, upon hearing his steps approaching the front door, it was almost without thinking that she donned the shell of the happy, easygoing Orlando.

When the door opened, she glanced over from where she sat on the sofa, a book in her hands that she hadn't been reading.

"Hi, hon," she said.

"Hi."

On the scale of Cranky Durrie to Stay-Away-at-All-Costs Durrie, he appeared closer to the former than the latter. Which was about the best she could hope for.

"How was your afternoon?"

"It was fine."

He walked toward the kitchen, undoubtedly to grab a beer. Before he got there, she said, "I was thinking about fish tacos. What do you say to hitting up Rubio's?"

It was one of his favorite places, not a random suggestion.

He stopped short of the kitchen entrance and looked over. "Yeah, I could do that."

They drove over to Rubio's on Grand Avenue, near the beach. While Durrie did the ordering, Orlando grabbed the last empty table outside. He brought the food out about five minutes later and set the tray on the table. After grabbing one of the cups of soda, Orlando dumped the contents into the landscaping separating the patio from the sidewalk. She covertly filled the cup with beer from a can she'd brought in her bag, and handed the cup to Durrie.

"Perfect," he said. "Thanks."

This was about as close as he'd been to a good mood as she'd seen in a long time.

After he finished his first taco and was about to start in on his second, she said, "More beer?"

"You brought two?"

"Please. I brought three."

He chuckled—also something she hadn't seen in ages—downed the last of his drink, and handed his cup to her.

She waited until he was halfway through his second cup before saying, "Quinn called."

Given Durrie's outburst after the Mexico City job, she assumed this would be the trickiest part of their conversation. But if the news affected him, it wasn't showing on his face.

"About the job?"

She nodded. "It's on."

He chomped off another bit of his taco and chewed it down. "Cool. When does he need me?"

"You're flying out on Tuesday."

Second taco done, Durrie picked up his third. "No clues on what the job is?"

"He didn't tell me, but he did want you to call him."

Durrie finished the taco and his beer without another word.

"You want some more?" she asked, nodding at his glass.

"I'm good. You feel like ice cream?"

The question caught her off guard, so it took her a moment before she said, "Sure."

They walked to the beach and picked up a couple of cones. Not once did either of them bring up the job again. In what was becoming a whole evening of surprises, Durrie actually took her hand when they reached the water.

Though she knew she shouldn't get her hopes up, she couldn't help but think maybe he'd turned a corner, and whatever demon he'd been struggling with was on its way out. Maybe, finally, the old Durrie would return, and she could fall in love with him all over again.

That night, as they lay in bed, Durrie said, "I'll call Quinn first thing in the morning. Get the details."

Orlando felt a wave of relief and wanted to throw her arms around him and hug him tight.

But again, not wanting to push him too much, she simply said a sleepy "Okay."

13

When Durrie called him, Quinn had asked if they could meet in person and said he could come down to San Diego.

"I wouldn't want to put you out," Durrie said. "I can come up there, if it's easier."

"I've already booked a flight for early this evening. How about grabbing dinner?"

"Sure. That sounds good."

"Is that hole-in-the-wall Italian place still in business?"

"Leonetti's? It is."

"Meet you there at eight?"

"I'll be there."

Quinn arrived at the restaurant fifteen minutes early, and was taken to the table he'd reserved near the back. It was the most private location, separated from the other customers by a wide aisle the servers used to go back and forth from the kitchen.

Durrie walked in at exactly eight p.m.

This was the first time Quinn had seen him in months, so his stomach clenched with trepidation of the man he feared Durrie had become. But that was the reason he'd wanted to have a face-to-face before the mission started. He didn't want to go in blind, and had decided to see first who he would be dealing with.

He caught his mentor's eye and waved him over. Putting on a smile, Quinn stood and held out his hand as Durrie approached.

"Hello, Johnny," Durrie said as they shook.

"Right on time. You look good."

"I look like shit and you know it." Durrie chuckled and sat down.

As Quinn retook his seat, a waitress approached. "Something to drink?"

"Definitely," Quinn said. He glanced back at the open menu on the table. "A Peroni, please."

"Sounds good to me, too," Durrie said.

The waitress smiled, said, "I'll be right back," and headed for the kitchen.

While waiting for their drinks, Quinn and Durrie perused their menus and covered all the small-talk bases.

How's San Diego?

Can't beat the weather. How's L.A.?

L.A.'s L.A. And Orlando? How's she doing?

Just fine. How's dating life?

What dating life?

Conversations like this were not something either of them was particularly good at, but they managed to stretch it out until the waitress returned, avoiding what would have surely been an awkward silence.

"Have you decided on what you'd like to order?"

Quinn went for the gnocchi with pesto sauce, while Durrie opted for the penne arrabbiata.

"So," Durrie said when they were alone again, "what's the deal with the job?"

"Standard clean. Travel day, two days on site, travel back."

"Cargo?" Durrie asked, meaning how many bodies they'd have to deal with.

"Five to ten."

Durrie's eyes widened. "Five to ten? And we only have a day to prep?"

"Disposal's already worked out. We'll just be delivering site to site."

"I see. Well, I guess that's better. Still a lot for just you and me to handle."

"It won't just be you and me. We'll have a driver who can also act as a third pair of hands."

"Oh, good. That's…that's good." Durrie paused. "If, uh, you haven't filled the position already, I met this guy I think you'd probably like working with. Angel Ortega. You know him?"

"I don't. But I've already got someone lined up."

"Figured you probably did. Who is it?"

"Trevor Hart."

Durrie furrowed his brow. "Was that the guy on that Grenada thing with us a few years ago?"

"No, he hasn't been around that long. You've probably never worked with him before but I've used him a few times. He's good. Listens to instructions."

Durrie smirked. "Unlike me."

"I wouldn't know. This is the first time…" Quinn trailed off, wishing he hadn't said that much.

"The first time you will be *my* boss?"

Quinn nodded.

"It's okay, Johnny. It's the way things go sometimes, you know. I…do appreciate you taking me on."

A part of Quinn wanted to tell him it hadn't been his choice to hire Durrie, but he kept that to himself. "Happy to have you on the team."

"You sure about that?"

"Of course."

That awkward silence they'd avoided finally caught up to them. Soon, their food arrived, and they were able to mask their lack of conversation as they dug into their meals.

It was Durrie who finally spoke again first. "Hey, uh, about the Mexico City job."

"You don't have to say anything. It got taken care of. Everything went fine."

"Yeah, Orlando told me. I just want you to know that I'm sorry I couldn't make it."

Quinn was pretty sure Durrie had never said *I'm sorry* to him before, not without irony anyway, and wasn't sure how to react.

Durrie saved him from having to do so by asking, "Who's our target?"

"That information will be distributed once the job starts."

"Seriously, Johnny? I'm not just some freelancer on his first gig."

Quinn grimaced. The stakes on this mission were high. They were going after a bin Laden associate. Peter's brief had stressed the information should be parsed out on a need-to-know basis. While Durrie would need to know eventually, he didn't need to now. But Durrie was also the man who had taught Quinn how to be a cleaner. Who, in the process, had shared secrets he probably shouldn't have. He had trusted Quinn, and Quinn owed him that.

In a low voice, Quinn said, "It's a man named El-Baz."

Durrie frowned and shook his head. "Never heard of him. What is he—Iraqi?"

"Saudi. You'll get the rest of the brief when we meet up."

"And when will that be?"

"Your flight leaves LAX at 12:20 a.m. on Tuesday."

"That's basically Monday night, not Tuesday."

"You'll have to take it up with the airlines. It's the best I could do. You'll arrive in San Juan, Costa Rica, the next morning, where I'll meet you at ten a.m. We have a private jet that will take us to our final destination."

"Which is?"

Quinn hesitated. "Rio."

"Rio, really? Okay, cool. That's a hell of a lot better than it could have been. But why are we meeting in Costa Rica and not just flying straight there?"

"Because that's where we're meeting."

"All right," Durrie said, raising his hands in surrender. "You're the lead. You know best."

By the time they finished eating, Quinn had allowed Durrie to tease out a few other, albeit minor, details from him. Quinn paid for the meal, and they headed outside to pick up their cars from the valet.

As they waited, Durrie said, "Thanks for coming down."

"My pleasure. It was good to see you again." The sentiment was genuine. The meeting had gone much better than Quinn had hoped. He had seen none of the problems he'd expected, and was beginning to think he'd been worried about nothing.

The valet pulled up in Durrie's car. Durrie took his keys and tipped the man, but instead of leaving, he turned to Quinn. "I need to ask you a favor."

"Um, sure."

"It's about Orlando."

"Orlando?"

"You're her best friend. If she needs anything, and I'm not there to help, you make sure she gets it."

Surprised by the request, it took Quinn a moment to realize what Durrie meant. If something happened to him, he wanted Quinn to take care of Orlando.

"You know I will," he said.

Durrie locked eyes with him, his expression turning dead serious. "By helping, I don't mean moving in. You get me?"

Quinn blinked. "I—"

"I'm not stupid. I know you love her, Johnny. But she'll always be mine. Understand?"

"Of course."

"Promise me."

A beat. "I promise."

Durrie relaxed, and his smile returned. "I'll see you on Tuesday."

"See you then."

Quinn watched Durrie drive away, feeling both guilty for his feelings toward Orlando and uneasy about Durrie's emotional swings.

14

Quinn's flight to San José, Costa Rica, left at 7:10 a.m.
Though he had implied to Durrie the trip had something to do with the El-Baz job, it did not. The truth was,
within a few hours he'd finished most of the prep work that could
be accomplished in California, the last item on his list being the
face-to-face with Durrie. Once that was all out of the way, he still
had two-plus days until he needed to head for Rio.

It seemed a waste to spend the time sitting around his Studio
City townhouse. The beach was still calling him. And while there
wasn't enough time to head back to the Mediterranean, there were
plenty of excellent alternatives between Los Angeles and Brazil.

There was one in particular that came to mind. He had booked
his ticket, and arranged for Durrie and Hart to meet him in Costa
Rica on the way to South America.

By the time Quinn picked up his rental car and navigated his
way west, to the village of Playa Agujas, it was after four p.m.

Though it wasn't a large town by any means, it took him forty
minutes to find the house he was looking for. Turned out he'd
driven by it three times, but because of a thick copse of trees in
front of it, he hadn't even realized a house was there until after he
finally stopped and asked a local for directions.

The house was smallish as far as beachside residences went, and looked quiet, like no one was home.

The only vehicle present when he drove up was a motorcycle sitting off to the side that could have been there for ten minutes or three years.

Quinn walked up to the front door and knocked.

Nothing. Not even the muffled steps of someone inside. The only thing he could hear was the waves on the other side of the house. He knocked again, but the door remained closed.

His instinct was to try the knob but this wasn't a job, and he had no need to enter without being invited. Besides, there were… other dangers to walking in unannounced.

He headed over to the carport and passed through it to a chest-high wall running along the back.

"Damn," Quinn whispered, impressed.

Directly behind the house was a large infinity pool that probably cost more than the home. Surrounding it, an expensive-looking wooden deck, populated with deck chairs and tables and a large outdoor kitchen. And on the opposite side of the deck from the house, framed by at least two dozen palm trees, sat ten meters of sandy beach and the Gulf of Nicoya.

After letting the beauty soak in for a moment, Quinn took a slower look around. A few towels lay in a crumpled pile on a lounge, and on the table beside it, a glass half filled with what looked like beer. There was no sign of who they belonged to, though.

Quinn entered the backyard through a wooden gate in the wall, and had his first look at the rear of the house. Smack dab in the center was a set of open, sliding glass doors. Through it, he could see an unoccupied living room.

Quinn took the three-tread staircase onto the deck and moved to the door, but remained outside.

"Anyone home?"

The house remained quiet.

He walked over to the lounge where the towels lay, and noted the condensation on the half-filled glass. The beer was still cold, so whoever it belonged to couldn't be too far away.

He looked to the beach, and then out into the ocean. It took a moment before he spotted a person swimming parallel to the sand, about thirty meters from shore.

There was a telescope just inside the house, but Quinn's personal code would not let him enter without permission. He jogged back to his car and retrieved the compact binoculars he kept in his backpack.

On the deck again, he aimed the glasses at the swimmer, and had to watch for a few strokes before the man turned his head to take a breath.

Quinn smiled. He was definitely in the right place.

It wasn't until the sun was almost touching the horizon that the swimmer finally headed to shore. When water became shallow enough for him to stand, he looked toward the house and paused, noticing he had a visitor.

He waded out of the ocean and crossed the sand, acting the part of an easygoing, nonthreatening vacationer. If Quinn had been a thug come to take advantage of a tourist, he would have been in for a big surprise when the approaching man inevitably turned the tables on him. But as soon as Quinn's friend drew close enough to see who was sitting on his deck, he laughed.

"Well, I'll be damned."

Quinn smiled. "Hello, Markoff."

"You get fired from a job again and suddenly have nothing to do?"

"Cute," Quinn said. He had never been fired in his life. "Actually, I've got a gig starting the day after tomorrow and this place just happens to be on the way, and I thought you were probably lonely so why not stop in and cheer you up."

Markoff smirked. "Oh, yeah. I've been hating life down here."

Quinn plucked one of the towels off the lounge and tossed it to his friend.

Markoff snagged it out of the air, said, "Thanks," and started to dry himself off. "I suppose you're going to want to stay here, too."

"If it's not too much trouble."

"It is, but I think I can fit you in." Markoff picked up his beer and downed what remained. "You hungry? There's a great seafood place not far down the road."

Quinn owed his life to Markoff.

A few years earlier, not long after Quinn had begun working on his own, Markoff had rescued him from having his throat cut by a Polish arms dealer. That was the first time they'd ever met.

Markoff was a field operative for the CIA, and after that first encounter, their paths had crossed again and again. Despite the fact Markoff was considerably more extroverted than Quinn—or maybe because of it—they had hit it off. They'd even taken a few vacations together and had a trip to Madagascar planned for later in the year.

When Markoff had headed to Costa Rica earlier in the month, on one of his frequent sabbaticals, he'd invited Quinn to join him. Quinn had thanked him, but his schedule had been too up in the air and he'd had to pass. But then this small window had opened.

Quinn had thought about letting his friend know he was on the way but decided to surprise him. If Markoff was busy, so be it; Quinn would have found someplace else to stay. But as he'd hoped, bunking at Markoff's place wouldn't be a problem.

They spent dinner reminiscing about jobs they'd worked together and people they knew in common. Not once did Markoff mention Durrie, a fact that in itself was telling. Markoff must've known Quinn's mentor was a delicate subject. Which meant he knew about the rumors swirling around Durrie. Markoff, more than anyone other than Orlando, was well aware of the complicated relationship Quinn had with his mentor.

After dinner, they walked back through town to Markoff's

place, grabbed several beers from the fridge, and went out to the deck, where the stars blazed overhead.

"It's worth the trip just for this," Quinn said, staring at the Milky Way.

"Dude, why do you think I came down here?"

Quinn smiled.

"If you tell anyone about this place, though, I'll kill you," Markoff said. "You know I can."

"I know you can try."

They fell into several moments of comfortable silence.

"So, this job you're on," Markoff said. "Anything I should know about?"

Quinn shook his head. "It's not happening in Costa Rica, if that's what you're worried about."

"Good," Markoff said, sounding relieved. "I wouldn't have been happy about that."

"I'm just meeting my team at the airport and we're flying on from here."

"Interesting. And you chose Costa Rica to stage from because…."

"Because I needed a little time on the beach."

"There are plenty of beaches in the world."

"But only one where I can get free room and board."

"I hate to break it to you, but that dinner is the only meal I'm paying for."

Quinn laughed and raised his glass. Markoff tapped it with his and they drank.

This time the quiet lasted for a good five minutes.

"Have you, um, seen Orlando lately?" Markoff asked.

Quinn kept his eyes aimed at the ocean as he lifted his beer back to his lips.

When he hadn't replied after several seconds, Markoff said, "Quinn, I know you. You don't drop in on people out of the blue. I'm guessing you came to talk. And usually that means you want to talk about her."

Markoff was the only one Quinn had ever told about his true feelings for Orlando. Quinn's friend was good at seeing through him, because Quinn, whether he wanted to admit it or not, *had* come here because of her.

"We did a job together a couple weeks ago, in Mexico City," Quinn said.

"Just the two of you?"

"On the clean team, yeah." Quinn hesitated. "It was supposed to be Durrie with me, but he...well, he couldn't make it at the last moment. You can't tell anyone that, though. Peter thinks he was with me the whole time."

"Excuse me?"

"It's complicated."

"You're telling me."

Markoff was waiting for Quinn to go on, but Quinn said nothing.

"Let's revisit that part later," Markoff said. "Tell me how things went with Orlando."

"Good. Nice and smooth."

"I'm not talking about the job."

Quinn snorted. "Also good. Great, even. It was like...before."

"Before?"

"Easy."

With Markoff's urging, Quinn told him about the mission and his time with Orlando, leaving out no details.

When he finished, Markoff shook his head, smirking.

"What?" Quinn asked.

"You're a good guy, Quinn."

"Um, thanks?"

"I didn't mean it as a compliment. You're the kind of good that gets in its own way."

"What the hell does that mean?"

Markoff looked at him for a moment, then out at the sea. "You kept the sheet between you."

"Well, yeah. What else was I supposed to do?"

"That's what I'm talking about. Let me ask you—what was the sheet supposed to block?"

"Something from happening."

"Between you."

"Obviously."

"So, if you hadn't put anything between you, are you saying you would have made a move on her?"

"What? No. Of course not."

"So then you're saying, she would have made a move on you."

"That's not what I meant, either. It's just..." Quinn trailed off, not sure what he meant.

"The point I'm trying make is that even if you didn't use the sheet as a wall, nothing would have happened."

"Well, okay. Yeah."

"But there's also this. Say Orlando might actually have been ready to, I don't know, move your relationship in a new direction. The sheet took that choice away from her, denying something I'm pretty sure you would have welcomed. *That's* what I mean by you're so good you can't get out of your own way."

Quinn frowned and finished off his beer. He hated his friend for confusing him like this.

Markoff let him cool off for a few minutes before saying, "Things between you two are...?"

"Good. You know, same as always."

Markoff laughed. "Which is it? Good, or same as always? It can't be both."

"Sure it can. She's my best friend."

"Who you love."

"Of course."

"As more than just a friend."

Quinn grabbed one of the unopened bottles, popped the top, and poured the beer in his glass.

"You still have never told her, have you?" Markoff asked.

"Are you crazy? Of course I haven't. She's in a relationship. That would be unfair. And probably the last time she talks to me."

Markoff shook his head again, then reached over and clapped Quinn on the back. "I do not envy you, my friend."

Both men took drinks, Quinn polishing off a good third of his glass in one go.

"You know, he's going on this job with me," Quinn said, his voice low.

"Who?" Markoff asked, then his eyes widened. "You mean Durrie?"

"He's my number two."

"Are you crazy? He flaked on you on the last job. And I'm sure you know that no one else is using him anymore."

"I owe him."

"Enough to risk getting yourself killed?"

"That's not going to happen."

Markoff rolled his eyes. "Admit it. You're really doing this for her."

"No. Not *just* for her. For both of them."

Markoff sighed. "You are a goddamn idiot, you know that? He was on a job for one of my contractors about nine months ago. Two people died because of his ineptness. Civilians, Quinn. Two *civilians*."

Quinn's brow furrowed. This was news to him. "What happened?"

"He was transporting the body to wherever the hell he was going to dump it and rushed a light. Unfortunately, there was a motorcycle cop waiting on the intersecting street, so naturally the cop pulled Durrie over. All Durrie had to do was act contrite, take his ticket, and be on his way. Instead, when the cop walked up to his window, Durrie shoved his van into reverse, backed into the cop's motorcycle, and then took off again. Since he wasn't sure if he disabled the bike or not, he laid on the speed and tried to get lost in the surrounding streets. One of his turns brought him face-to-face with a sedan coming in the other direction. The other driver swerved to miss Durrie, but that sent him straight into a bus stop on the corner. One of the people waiting there died on impact, another a few hours later in the hospital. Four additional people, including the driver, were seriously injured.

"Durrie is a walking disaster. If you're smart, you'd cancel him right now. Look, I still have a week of vacation left, but if you need someone to replace him, I'll do it. Free of charge."

Quinn stared into his beer. After a few moments, he said, "I appreciate the offer. Really."

"But you're not going to take me up on it."

"I can't."

"I hate to sound like a broken record, but if you wanted another example of being too good to get out of your own way, this is it."

"I'd be nothing if not for him."

"That's not true."

"No. It is. Literally. I'd be dead."

"You'd be dead if not for me, too."

"Exactly. And I'd do whatever I needed to help you, too."

Now it was Markoff's turn to fall silent. Finally he said, "He could very well get you killed. Which would mean he didn't really save your life before. He just put off your termination date for a few years."

"That's not fair."

"Isn't it?"

Quinn didn't reply.

Taking a more conciliatory tone, Markoff said, "I know I'm not going to be able to talk you out of this. Just promise me you'll keep a sharp eye on him, and you won't give him anything important to do."

Quinn took a breath. "I promise."

15

Quinn woke to the smell of frying bacon. He wandered out of the guest bedroom and found Markoff sipping coffee in the kitchen.

"Hungry?" Markoff asked.

"Not really." A significant portion of last night's dinner still sat in Quinn's stomach.

"Come on. You're on vacation."

"For one day."

"Your loss," Markoff said as he removed the bacon from the pan. "Thought maybe we'd head out in thirty minutes. Okay by you?"

"Head out where?"

Markoff smiled. "You'll see."

"You know how I love surprises," Quinn said, deadpan.

After grabbing some clothes from his bag, he went into the guest bath and took a shower. When he came back out, Markoff had retreated to his own room to get ready. While Quinn waited, he opened his computer to make sure Peter hadn't sent any changes to the job.

There was a handful of messages, but none from Peter. One, however, was from Trevor Hart. Quinn clicked on it.

"Son of a bitch."

"What was that?" Markoff called from the other room.

"What? Oh, nothing."

It wasn't nothing.

Quinn,

I hate to be so last minute with this, but I'm not going to be able to make the job tomorrow. My parents were in an accident. Nothing life threatening, but they're both in the hospital. I need to go help them. I hope you understand.

I'm so sorry.

Trevor

As annoying as it was to lose a team member the day before a mission, he couldn't be mad at Trevor. Under similar circumstances, Quinn would have done the same thing. Well, for his mom, anyway. His stepdad would have been a different matter.

Now he had to find a replacement, and quick.

Orlando was the obvious choice. But what if he had to reprimand Durrie in front of her? Durrie would not take that well, and who knows how Orlando would react. And how would they work together? What if there was tension for some reason?

No, Orlando was not an option.

What about Markoff? He had offered to fill in for Durrie but having him take Trevor's spot was a bad idea, too. If Orlando working beside Durrie was the last thing Quinn wanted, then Markoff doing the same was the second to last. Quinn knew Markoff well enough to realize his friend would have an extremely difficult time not calling Durrie out on his bullshit, no matter how small. And that could send the mission south in a heartbeat. If Durrie caused any problems, Quinn wanted to be the one who dealt with it, no one else.

He started going down his list of preferred operatives, texting each and asking about his or her availability.

Markoff walked into the living room, wearing board shorts and an unbuttoned yellow cotton shirt. "Ready?"

Quinn glanced up from his phone. "I'm going to need just a bit."

"Something wrong?"

"A minor hiccup."

"The job?"

"Uh-huh."

"Anything I can do to help?"

Quinn shook his head. "Just waiting to hear back."

"Which you could do *anywhere*."

Quinn looked at him and laughed. "You're right."

"Then let's go."

It turned out the man who had rented the house to Markoff owned a speedboat called the *Belle Michelle* that Markoff had access to.

Quinn and Markoff cruised into the Gulf of Nicoya, where they sped around for a couple of hours before heading over to the peninsula across the way for lunch.

Everyone at the restaurant seemed to know Markoff. He was that kind of guy.

Sometimes Quinn wished he could be more relaxed and easier to talk to, like his friend. Relaxing for Quinn took work, which kind of defeated the purpose. And as far as being easy to talk to, he was fine with people he knew, not so great with those he didn't. When he was being himself, he was too self-conscious. The only time he could escape a tied-up tongue was on a job requiring him to play the role of someone else.

They were led to a table overlooking the dock where the *Belle Michelle* was secured.

"The usual?" the waiter asked in Spanish.

"Yes, Ramon. For each of us," Markoff replied in kind. He looked at Quinn as the waiter walked off. "You're going to love this. Best ceviche I've ever had."

"High praise, coming from you." Quinn looked around. "Is there a toilet here?"

Markoff point toward the entrance. "Back around the bar. You'll see it."

"Thanks," Quinn said as he stood up.

He had felt the first of the replies to his text come in not long after he and Markoff first headed into the bay, and vibrating notifications had been trickling in ever since. He'd been hesitant to check them in front of Markoff, knowing his friend would again offer his services. So, he'd decided to wait until he could get a moment alone.

Not surprisingly, the majority of his contacts were already out on other jobs. He'd been prepared for that, which was why he'd cast his net wider than usual. What he hadn't been prepared for was that those who weren't working had been put on hold for one project or another, preventing them from taking Quinn's gig.

Dammit.

What the hell was he going to do now?

He looked back toward the restaurant. He might have to ask Markoff after all. He checked his email to see if Peter had sent the final go/no-go yet. But the only email he'd received since he last checked was from Durrie.

Wanted to let you know I'll be flying from San Diego to LAX at 7 p.m., so will have no problem making the midnight flight. After last time, didn't want you to think I wouldn't be there.

It was unexpectedly responsible, and made Quinn wonder if that intense moment they'd had in front of Leonetti's had been an aberration, and that maybe his initial feeling that Durrie was starting to turn a corner was accurate.

He exited the bathroom, but instead of returning to the table, he slipped out the front door onto the quiet street, walked a dozen meters away to where he wouldn't be overheard by anyone, and called Peter.

"What is it?" Peter asked. "Is there a problem?"

"Just wondering where we are on the mission. My people are

scheduled to start moving out tonight, but I haven't received the final go from you yet."

"Because I don't know it yet. Intelligence indicates everything's still on track, but it's the kind of thing that could change at any moment. You and your team should head down, though. If we have to cancel once you're there, so be it."

"All right. Then I'll consider us on."

"Anything else?"

"No, that's it."

After they said their goodbyes, Quinn started walking back to the restaurant, racking his brain on how he was going to fill Hart's spot. After a few meters, he stopped.

Durrie had mentioned an operative he'd worked with. Something Ortega. Quinn thought for a moment. Angel. Angel Ortega. Quinn didn't know the guy, but Ortega shouldn't be too hard to check out.

He emailed an info broker he knew and asked for a background check on Durrie's friend, saying he would pay extra for a rush. He then called Durrie.

"Your friend Ortega, can you give me his number?"

"Sure," Durrie said, sounding surprised. "Are you thinking about hiring him?"

"Thinking about it. Nothing definite."

"Peter letting us have a fourth man?"

Quinn hesitated before saying, "Hart can't make it."

"Oh. Sorry to hear that. Well, if you do call Angel, I'm sure you'll like him." He gave Quinn the number. "If that doesn't work, let me know. Otherwise, I'll see you tomorrow."

"See you then."

Ortega answered on the third ring.

"Hello?"

"Angel Ortega? This is Jonathan Quinn. I got your number from Durrie."

A brief pause. "Right. He did say a few days ago he might mention me to you. What can I do for you?"

"I know this is kind of last minute, but are you available for the next four to five days?"

"Just finished up something on Friday and my next job's not for another two weeks so, yeah, I'm free."

"Great. To be clear, this isn't an official booking yet. I'd like to put you on hold, and should be able to give you the final word in three hours or so. If I do hire you, I'll need you in Costa Rica tomorrow by ten a.m. Where are you located?"

"Las Vegas."

"Perfect. If you can get to LAX this evening, I can book you on the flight leaving not long after midnight."

"Plenty of flights between here and there. You give me the okay, and I'll be on one of them."

"Thanks, I'll let you know."

Given that Ortega had been Durrie's recommendation, Quinn had been concerned the man would be a little off. But the operative had come across as normal, at least in their short conversation. If the report on him came back clean, maybe everything would work out after all.

He headed back into the restaurant.

"Where the hell have you been?" Markoff asked after Quinn sat down.

"Sorry. Needed to make a call."

Markoff studied him for a moment. "You sure you don't need my help with anything?"

"Nope. I've got it all handled."

"All right. If you say so." Markoff raised one of the two glasses of beer that had been brought out. "Here's to no more business."

Ortega's report arrived in Quinn's inbox twenty minutes before he and Markoff returned to the house. After reading it, whatever remaining concerns he'd had about Ortega disappeared. By all accounts, the man was a competent, albeit relatively new, operative. He should do just fine.

Quinn called Ortega and finalized the details, then sent Durrie a text letting him know his friend had been hired and would be flying out on the same Costa Rica-bound jet that night.

Work finally dealt with, Quinn joined Markoff for a walk into town for dinner, this time to a restaurant with a deck overlooking the water. They ate red snapper and drank Pilsen beer, while taking turns telling stories of crazy things that had happened to them in the field.

From the restaurant it was a short walk down the beach to a bar called Pasco Azul, where a real-life scene from the old TV show *Cheers* played out as soon as they walked in.

The bartender, an attractive thirtysomething woman in a T-shirt that read MY PLACE MY RULES, called out, "*Hola*, Mickey."

As a card-carrying member of the CIA, Markoff never traveled anywhere under his real name. He was using the alias Mickey Carter on this trip.

Most of the customers sitting at the bar offered similar greetings. Markoff and Quinn took two stools among them, and the bartender plopped down a Pilsen and a glass in front of Markoff.

"You the same?" she asked Quinn, in thickly accented English.

"*Por favor.*"

She smiled and placed the same in front of him.

"Who's your friend?" she asked Markoff.

"This asshole? This is…" Though he and Quinn had not discussed an alias for Quinn, he hesitated no more than half a second before saying, "Thomas Wright. You can call him Tommy." He turned to Quinn. "Tommy, this is Marta. She owns the place."

When Marta held out her hand, Quinn wasn't sure if he should kiss it or shake it. Fortunately, Marta took charge of the situation and shook his hand.

"Nice to meet you, Tomás," she said, a twinkle in her eye.

"You, too," Quinn said.

When she left to help another customer, Quinn leaned over

and whispered to Markoff, "Tommy Wright? You couldn't have come up with something a little better?"

The choice of Tommy Wright had not been random. They both knew an operative by that name, a guy who, though well meaning, always seemed to say something that rubbed someone else the wrong way. Each of them had told a story about him at dinner.

"It's a fine name." Markoff raised his glass and held it toward Quinn. "To Tommy Wright, wherever the hell he may be."

Quinn rolled his eyes and touched his glass to Markoff's. "To Tommy."

It turned out Markoff was passing himself off to the locals as an extreme adventure guide, who would, for a price, take clients anywhere in the world they wanted to go, whether or not they were legally allowed to be there. This gave him the opportunity to regale them with made-up tales, loosely based on some of his real-world exploits, a few of which he told that night at the bar.

It was an approach that made Quinn uncomfortable. He was a strict what-happens-on-the-job-stays-on-the-job kind of person. Markoff taking things right up to the edge of reality made Quinn want to look around every few minutes to make sure a CIA internal investigation unit wasn't busting into the bar, ready to hustle everyone off to Guantanamo Bay.

But Marta kept serving up the beers, and soon Quinn forgot about a potential prison sentence. He even joined in now and then with the laughter at Markoff's faux adventures.

At some point, he told himself he should stop drinking. The mission was starting tomorrow, and he would be meeting Durrie and Ortega in San José at ten. But Marta was persistent, always setting a new bottle in front of him before he emptied his glass.

While Markoff carried on entertaining the masses, at one point Marta and Quinn began their own side conversation. The bartender moved her stool directly across from him on the other side of the bar. With Markoff's booming narration, the laughter of his audience, and the music that had been playing all evening, it was only natural that Quinn and Marta leaned closer and closer together to be heard.

"I see Los Angeles on TV," she said, scrunching up her face. "Very big. I do not like it."

He probably shouldn't have told her he lived in L.A. but what the hell, it wasn't the same as giving her a blow-by-blow of his latest job, a la Markoff.

"I don't mind it," he said. "Great weather. Good food."

"Here is great weather and *great* food. Why I want to share these with a million others?"

"It's a bit more than a million."

"More reason to stay here, yes?"

He smiled and took another drink.

"Your family there?" she asked.

"Los Angeles? No."

"Your job, then. This is why you live there."

"Um, not really."

"Then why you not live someplace like here?"

Quinn opened his mouth to give her some lame answer about how he liked L.A. and was happy there, but she cut him off.

"I know. You have wife there."

Quinn held up his left hand and wiggled his ringless fingers. "No wife."

She snorted. "Men do not always wear the ring."

"No wife," he repeated.

"Girlfriend, then. Yes. Maybe more than one?"

Quinn laughed. "No girlfriend, either."

Her brow furrowed. "Boyfriend?"

"Not my thing."

"You are alone? Why? You a nice man. Handsome."

"Thank you." He picked up his glass again and downed what was left.

Marta reached under the bar and pulled up a full bottle she had waiting there.

As she started to open it, Quinn said, "I think I've had

enough." He didn't have to get out of his chair to know he hadn't been this drunk in a long time.

But Marta popped the top and refilled his glass.

"Okay, but this is my last one," he said.

"We'll see."

Their eyes locked for a few moments before Quinn forced himself to look away.

"You're a strange man, Tomás."

He laughed and took a sip of his beer, not sure how to respond.

"Tell me, do you like my bar?"

He glanced around. "Yeah. It's great. Who doesn't love a bar on the beach?"

"And me?"

"I'm sorry?" he said, not understanding what she meant.

She reached across the short distance between them and pulled his head toward hers, her lips finding his. Quinn held still for a moment, not quite realizing what was going on. When he figured it out, he knew he should pull back, but instead he found his lips opening and felt her tongue slip into his mouth.

It had been a long, long time since he last kissed someone, and he could feel his body surging with hunger, a need, a desire for more. He couldn't have pulled away if he tried.

"Oh, my." It was Markoff's voice, but Quinn barely heard it at first. "You two need some help? You appear to have gotten stuck together."

Quinn froze, his lips still on Marta's. Sensing his discomfort, Marta pulled away. She smiled sheepishly as Quinn smiled back, tentative and a bit embarrassed.

"Hey, I didn't mean to stop anything," Markoff said.

Quinn turned and saw that Markoff and the others were all looking at him and Marta. The room wavered around them, and Quinn had to press his hand against the bar to keep from falling off his chair.

A million thoughts flooded his mind.

The kiss.
The job.
Orlando.
The drive back to San José.
Durrie and Ortega.
Marta.
Orlando.
The beer.
Markoff.
Orlando.

"I think I should probably get to bed," he said.

Markoff grinned. "Don't let me stop you."

"At *your* place." Quinn stared at Markoff, silently reminding his friend they had arrived together.

Markoff sighed. "Right. Okay. Marta, what do we owe you?"

She held out her hand. "Give me your key."

His eyes narrowed. "You want my house as payment? How much did we drink? And you know I don't own that place, right?"

"You are very funny," she said, not laughing. "I will help your friend go home. You can enjoy your evening a little longer."

Markoff sighed. "I should really do it."

"It is no problem." She looked at one of the others sitting at the counter. "Diego, you bartend until I get back."

A young man who couldn't have been much over twenty jumped off his stool and headed around the bar.

Marta looked back at Markoff, her hand still extended. "Well?"

He looked at her for a moment, and then pulled a key ring with a single key on it out of his pocket and set it in her hand. "Be gentle with him."

Quinn didn't quite remember leaving the bar. One moment he was sitting on a stool, and the next he was walking on the beach, leaning against Marta. He could hear the waves breaking several meters to their left, but the moon had yet to rise, so all he could see was an undulating sheet of black where the ocean was.

The water did seem to be getting closer, though.

"Whoa," Marta said, gently pushing him away from the waves. "Better to keep your eyes ahead."

"Sorry."

"It's okay." She smiled at him. "You do not drink much, do you?"

"I drink," he said. "I just don't drink *that* much."

"So, you're saying it is my fault."

He looked at her, which caused him to lurch toward the water again. He turned back forward before they could deviate too much from their path.

"As a matter of fact, I guess it would be your fault." This is what he intended to say. His words, however, came out a bit more slurred. But apparently he got his meaning across.

"You're right. *Lo siento.*"

"You're forgiven."

"That is very kind of you."

"I can be…kind now and then," he said.

"I think more often than that."

They walked on in silence, the warm night breeze feeling good against his skin. The wind, however, wasn't the only thing touching him. Marta was pressed against his left side, her arm stretched across his back, while his arm lay across her shoulders. He could feel her hand hugging his ribs. It was then that he realized her left hand was spread against his chest to keep him from falling forward, her fingers moving in a slow circle, as if she was massaging him.

Or caressing.

"It's, uh, very nice of you to do this. I mean it."

"It's nothing."

"It's not nothing."

She pressed her head against his shoulder.

He liked it, and yet he didn't. He frowned. That wasn't true. He liked it, but didn't want to. It troubled him because he had a feeling the reason he liked it had more to do with the physical contact than the person giving it to him. Marta seemed nice—really nice, actually—but who he wished was holding him up was nearly three thousand miles away.

"Careful," Marta said.

Quinn blinked and looked down. They were at the edge of a stone walkway that looked exactly like the walkway behind Markoff's house. He tilted his head up.

Oh.

It *was* the walkway behind Markoff's house. They had arrived a lot faster than he'd expected. Or had he blacked out again?

Marta guided him along the stones onto the deck, and to the sliding doors at the back of the house, where she leaned him against the wall. "Don't fall."

"I'll try not to."

She unlocked the door, slid it open, and helped Quinn inside.

"You are using the guest room, yes?" she asked.

"Yes. It's back over—"

"I know where it is."

He raised an eyebrow, a move considerably more exaggerated than it would have been if he was sober.

"Don't look at me like this," she said. "I have been in many of the houses here. When people throw a party, they need a bartender. Many times, this is me."

"Right. I guess that makes sense."

"You want me to drop you here or take you to your bed?"

"Uh…uh…" Quinn had no idea how to respond without it coming out wrong.

She laughed and took him into his bedroom. After helping him sit on the bed, she started taking off his shirt.

"I can do it," he said, but by that time she already had it over his head and off.

"Stand up," she told him.

He rose unsteadily to his feet, and she started unbuckling his belt. He reached down to do it himself, but again was too late. When the zipper was down, she yanked his pants toward the ground while mercifully leaving his underwear in place.

She pulled the sheet back from the bed. "In, please."

He hesitated. "I-I can't do this."

"You can't get in bed?"

"I can't do *this*." He motioned back and forth between them. "I'm sorry. I…shouldn't have led you on."

"You think I'm getting in bed with you?" Another laugh. "No, I am not."

"Oh."

She nodded at the bed expectantly.

"Right."

After he climbed in, she pulled the sheet over him and knelt down next to the mattress.

"And you did not lead me on. I kissed *you*, remember?"

"I seem to recall something about that."

"Who is Orlando?"

He tensed. "Excuse me?"

"When we were walking, I could hear you saying the name to yourself."

"Oh."

"Is Orlando a man or a woman?"

"She-she's a woman."

"But not your girlfriend."

"No."

"Do you want her to be?"

This time, Quinn mustered enough energy to resist answering.

Marta smiled again, then ran a finger along the bridge of his nose. "You are very…desirable."

He remained quiet.

She studied his face for several more seconds, and stood back up. "I should get back. I hope I see you at the bar again."

"Me, too."

She walked to the door, stopped, and looked back. "Does she know that you are in love with her?"

He took a breath. "No."

"You should tell her."

And with that, she left.

16

"You have everything?" Orlando asked, eyeing the small bag Durrie was carrying.

"This is it," he said. "Should be done by Friday, so don't need that much."

She nodded. "I'm sure it's going to go great."

"Of course it is. Why wouldn't it?"

"I'm just saying, that's all." She brushed a piece of lint off his shirt. "Don't give Quinn a hard time."

Durrie snorted. "He's the boss. I'm contractually obligated not to give him a hard time."

She threw her arms around him. "Be careful."

"You shouldn't worry so much."

"I'll try to remember that." She kissed his cheek. "I'm…proud of you."

His instinct was to stiffen and say, "Proud of what? That I'm doing my job?" But he caught himself before she could sense his reaction and stayed silent.

She kissed him again, this time on the mouth. He made his lips soft, letting her take the lead. It was important that she thought everything was fine.

When she pulled away, she said, "Let me know how you're doing, if you get a chance."

"I will."

"And remember, if you guys need anything, I'm just a phone call away."

"Thanks, hon. I'll let Quinn know." He wouldn't.

She looked him over, sizing him up. "I feel like I'm sending you off to school."

He had the same feeling, but not in the pleasant way she meant.

"I'll see you Friday, Saturday latest," he said.

"I'll be here."

He entered the garage and climbed into his car. As he backed down the driveway and pulled onto the street, he could sense her watching him from the living room window. He didn't check, though. Orlando, their house, and everything both represented was in his past now. This evening marked the start of a new era.

An era in which he would control every aspect of his life.

Making arrangements for Trevor Hart to be suddenly unavailable for the job had been child's play. A call to a morally questionable fixer Durrie knew had done the trick.

"Don't make it too dramatic," he had told the man. "No one dies, but at least one should stay in the hospital for a day or two."

"You got it."

The man had not failed him.

Removing the other operatives on Quinn's go-to list from contention had been a bit more difficult, only due to the number. Durrie had spent an entire afternoon making phone calls and putting people on fictitious holds.

The wild card had always been getting Quinn to hire Ortega. Durrie knew Quinn, knew how his old apprentice's mind worked, and knew presenting Ortega as a potential team member, if the need arose, would require a delicate touch. Too heavy-handed and Quinn would've been suspicious of Durrie's motive. Too light a push and Quinn might've taken it as a tacit devaluation of Ortega's abilities. The key was to drop his new protégée's name and throw in a few honest-sounding comments about the man's strengths, so that Ortega's name would remain in Quinn's mind.

Even then, that was not a guarantee Quinn would call Ortega when all his normal contacts proved unavailable. For this, Durrie had been counting on two things. First, that Quinn's sense of obligation to help Durrie would make him think hiring Ortega was a vote of confidence in his mentor. Second, that the mere idea of showing faith in Durrie would please Orlando, even if she never found out about the hiring. This was likely the stronger motivation.

Durrie sometimes imagined Quinn as a reincarnation of a chivalrous knight—probably more the fictional kind than the actual—who performed acts of duty or kindness with no thought to whether or not anyone knew about his deeds, or how such deeds might affect him.

It was a bullshit code of ethics, as far as Durrie was concerned. There may have been a time when he'd been more inclined to understand Quinn's actions, even if he wouldn't have undertaken them himself. But he'd eventually seen through the crap and realized it was an act, the self-flagellation of one's ego. And whatever "honor" Quinn thought he gained from acting this way was a lie he told himself to pretend it wasn't a flaw in his character.

But a flaw for one man was an opportunity for another. And damn if Durrie's exploitation of Quinn's flaw hadn't worked perfectly.

When Ortega had called to tell him he'd been hired to fill the empty slot, Durrie was rendered momentarily speechless.

"You still there?" Ortega had said.

"Yeah. Still here."

"So, are we going to do it? Or have you changed your mind?"

"We're doing it. Hang tight. I need to make some calls."

Now here he was, sitting on a red-eye flight to Costa Rica, Ortega two rows behind him, speeding headlong toward his self-changed destiny.

Durrie wasn't sure he had ever been so happy in his life.

17

Quinn clutched the wheel and stared ahead, using more energy than normal to focus on the road to San José.

It could have been worse, he supposed. Markoff's hangover remedy—a smoothie containing coconut, banana, pineapple, some yogurt, and a couple of raw eggs—and the four aspirin Quinn had washed down with it had taken the edge off his headache. But the general sense of being reanimated roadkill refused to go anywhere.

It wasn't until he reached the airport outside the Costa Rican capital that he could claim to be half human again.

What had he been thinking? He always tried to have a quiet evening the night before a mission. Even if he went out, he would never have more than a drink or two and would be in bed at a decent hour. But now he'd broken that rule twice in one month. And last night had been magnitudes worse than his evening out with Orlando in Mexico City.

He could recall only bits and pieces of his walk back to Markoff's place with Marta, and was pretty sure that without her, he would have washed up on the beach this morning, another overindulging tourist killed by his own stupidity.

He could kid himself and say he'd had a few too many

because he was having a good time, that he wasn't paying attention. Or he could be honest and admit that his desire for a loss of control had been building in him for a while. A release, if you will. From his concerns about Durrie, yes, but mostly from his frustration with his feelings for Orlando.

To that end, perhaps the evening hadn't been a total disaster. Seeing everything through the pain-inducing sunlight of morning, he couldn't deny the futility of his feelings for her. It was time for him to move on. Details on how to achieve that goal to be worked out later.

With an hour and a half to kill until his rendezvous with Durrie and Ortega, Quinn hunted down a mild breakfast of dry toast and unseasoned eggs, and then proceeded to the offices of the private jet company taking his team to Rio. After a quick meeting with the owner, who would also be serving as pilot, Quinn was escorted to the hangar by a young male assistant. Sitting beside the aircraft were the two containers of special cargo Peter had arranged to be delivered.

The assistant retreated to the side of the hangar, leaving Quinn to inspect the gear in private. Using the digital code Peter had given him, Quinn unlocked the first box. Inside, he found six pistols, a collapsible rifle, a shotgun, spare mags for the pistols and rifle, ammo, sound suppressors, and a box of ten flash-bang grenades.

Box two contained nine comm sets, two extra sets for each team member in case of malfunction; an electronics detector; an alarm detector; tracking chips; audio bugs; rope; zip ties; and duct tape. If all went according to plan, most of the supplies would not be needed, but it was always better to be prepared. He resealed the boxes and signaled to the assistant to return. Together they loaded the boxes into the jet.

Quinn proceeded to the rendezvous point, where, despite the fact there were still twenty minutes until meeting time, Durrie and Ortega sat waiting. When Durrie noticed Quinn walking up, he pushed to his feet and smiled. Following Durrie's lead, Ortega did the same.

"Morning, Johnny," Durrie said. As Quinn drew closer, his smile faltered a little. "You look like crap. Are you all right?"

"A bad meal," Quinn said. "I'll be fine."

"That sucks." Durrie held out his hand. "Good to see you, though."

Quinn shook with him. Durrie seemed like the old Durrie again, the surly mentor who had expertly guided Quinn's training.

"Have you met Angel yet?" Durrie said, nodding at the third member of the team.

"Only on the phone." Quinn shook hands with Ortega. "I appreciate you being able to join us on short notice."

"No problem. Happy I could help."

"Tell me, Johnny, what time does our plane leave?" Durrie asked.

"As soon as we board."

"Private jet?" When Quinn nodded, Durrie's smile broadened. "I like the sound of that."

The flight to Rio was uneventful. Quinn spent most of the time going back over the mission brief, making sure he had every detail memorized, and all contingencies accounted for.

He was more nervous than usual. While he'd been running his own operations for a few years now, and successfully so, anytime he and Durrie had been on a job together, Durrie had been lead. With their roles reversed, Quinn couldn't help but feel like he was the one being judged instead of the other way around.

On the surface, the mission was straightforward. One, load the bodies into a transport van. Two, clean the scene. Three, deliver the bodies to the plane, and strap them into the seats they would "die" in during the crash. Four, clean the van. Five, go home.

The only potential complication was the number of targets. Six on the low end, eleven on the high. If the strike team was unable to subdue all of El-Baz's security detail, some of the agents might be killed, too, upping the body count. This was one of those contingencies Quinn and his team needed to prepare for. Standard procedure for any operative killed during a mission was that he or she would be processed in country. In other words, the agent's body would also need to disappear.

Quinn couldn't put any dead friendlies on the plane with El-Baz and his people, however. Though the plane was to be ditched in the middle of the ocean, there was always the chance it would eventually be discovered. If extra bodies were found on board, the idea that the crash had been an accident wouldn't hold up for long.

A separate method would be needed, which meant adding a step to Quinn's to-do list. During his prep work before he left Los Angeles, he'd researched the viability of implementing several of his go-to methods in Rio, and had been pleased to find he had some excellent choices. After talking to a few people he trusted who had experience in the Brazilian city, he settled on a mortuary with an owner who was known to help out in the war on terror when needed.

The team's jet was still two hours from Rio when Quinn finally shut his computer and leaned back. Behind him, he could hear Ortega's deep, slumbering breaths. The man had fallen asleep minutes after takeoff and hadn't stirred since.

Durrie had also passed out not long after wheels up, but now, when Quinn looked in his direction, Durrie was sitting up, looking out the window. He must have sensed Quinn's attention, because after a couple of moments, Quinn's mentor looked over his shoulder.

"Hey, Johnny. All done boning up?"

It was a trick question. Durrie lesson number 17: You can never be too prepared.

"Just taking a break," Quinn said.

Durrie smiled. "Words starting to melt together, are they?"

"A little."

"I've been thinking. After this job, I'd be happy to work under you again."

"Oh, um, okay. That's good to hear."

"I guess what I'm saying is, you're giving me a chance, and I want you to know I appreciate that."

"You're welcome."

"You got something lined up after this? Something you can slot me in for?"

Quinn wasn't sure he was ready to talk about future work yet. "Let me take a look at things and I'll let you know."

"Sure, Johnny. Just wanted to throw that out there." Durrie turned back to the window, making Quinn think that was the end of the conversation. But after a lengthy pause, his mentor said, "There's a whole lot of world out there."

"There sure is, isn't there?" Quinn said.

"Hard to find a place to be alone anymore, though. People are everywhere."

Quinn said nothing, not sure where this was going.

"You remember that first time you went with me to Rio?"

"Of course." Quinn had been Durrie's apprentice for only a few months, and it had been his first time crossing the equator.

"That had been a little messy. But not our fault."

"No, not ours."

A hit on a Rwandan war criminal who had escaped justice for far too long. The target sensed the trap and tried to escape, making it out of a building and onto a dark and all but deserted side street where he shot a woman and stole her car. Before he could pull away, a bullet to the back of his head from the assassin put an end to his freedom.

It was the civilian Durrie was talking about, though.

Quinn was the first to reach her. She was twenty-three and had just finished a shift on the last of three jobs she worked every day to support her family. Those, of course, were details Quinn learned later. Something he figured out at the scene was that the war criminal's bullet had missed her heart but clipped an artery, leaving her to bleed out.

Though it was a fruitless task, Quinn kept pressure on both the entry and exit wounds.

"Let her go, Johnny," Durrie had said.

"Call an ambulance!" Quinn said.

"There's no coming back from where she's going. Leave her be."

This was the first time Quinn had seen this side of his mentor. Though it was the practical response, to Quinn it felt heartless.

The girl, her eyes wide in fear, whispered something.

Quinn leaned his ear toward her mouth. "Say it again."

This time he heard her, but her words were in Portuguese, a language that—at the time—Quinn didn't understand. In the coming months, her native tongue became the first of many languages he would learn.

Her voice became softer and softer as she kept repeating herself, until the only sound was that of her lips tapping against each other. And then even that stopped. Moments later, her heart beat for the last time.

When the fear in her eyes turned into a cold, lifeless stare, he knew he had failed.

"Clean yourself up, then bag her," Durrie said, dropping a body bag beside the dead woman.

Quinn looked up. "What are we going to do with her?"

"You know the protocol."

Quinn did. All deaths associated with the Rwandan's assassination were to be cleaned. It had seemed a logical directive, but he had never truly thought it would include someone like her.

"She must have family. How are they going to find out?"

"No idea. I just know they're not going to find out from us. Do the job."

As respectfully as possible, Quinn bagged her, and then helped Durrie do the same with the Rwandan. Both bodies went in the trunk of the woman's car, since the vehicle, too, needed to be disposed of.

On the flight home, Durrie told Quinn that in cases like this, families were often compensated by whoever had ordered the hit. That did little to quell the unease in Quinn's mind. After they arrived back in the States, he had come close to quitting.

Two things had kept him from doing so. The first was the fact that, by offering him the apprenticeship, Durrie had stayed the hands of the powers that be from terminating Quinn. If he'd left so soon after beginning this new life, there was every chance his death sentence would've been reinstated.

But the main reason he'd decided not to walk away was the death of the woman, and his desire to prevent something similar from ever happening again. He knew Durrie would never care, but Quinn would. He would do everything in his power to help any innocent victims survive.

If Durrie had known about this, he would have scoffed and said it was a stupid vow made by an innocent punk. And yet, after Quinn's five-year internship and now his time on his own, it was still one of the guiding principles he lived by.

No, the woman's death in Rio had not been Durrie and Quinn's fault. It had just always felt that way.

"Any chance this gig is going to be as messy as that one?" Durrie asked.

"The location is isolated, so hopefully not," Quinn said.

Durrie grunted and nodded, and said something that startled Quinn. "You were right to try to save her, you know. Not sure if I ever told you that."

It took Quinn a moment to find his voice. "No...you never did."

Another grunt. "Well, you were."

Quinn glanced away for a moment, then said, "Thank you."

A gray SUV—not too old, not too new—awaited Quinn and his team at the hangar in Rio. They loaded the trunks into the back and drove to their hotel in the city, five kilometers from where the job would take place.

Their adjoining rooms were on the twelfth floor, facing Guanabara Bay—Quinn in his own room, Durrie and Ortega sharing the other.

After they were settled, Durrie stepped through their shared doorway and said, "Angel and I thought we'd go out and grab some dinner. Want to join us?"

"I've got a few things I need to take care of first," Quinn said. "Text me where you end up, and if it doesn't take me too long, I'll come over."

Smirking, Durrie said, "You know, all that extra work is the one thing I don't miss about being the boss."

After they left, Quinn stared out the window for a few minutes. If anything, he was more confused than ever about how he should feel about Durrie. First, there were the rumors and the warnings from Peter, and the stories from Orlando. Then there was the missed job in Mexico. All of which had soured his already skeptical view of his former teacher.

But then there had been the meeting at Leonetti's. Durrie attentive, engaged, almost contrite. Yes, there was that moment at the end that had been out of character for the evening. But the more Quinn thought about it, the more he felt it was simply a veteran agent wanting to make sure the woman he loved was taken care of if something happened to him. His admonition to Quinn a cover for his fear of failure. But since they had rendezvoused in San José, Durrie had been nothing but friendly and respectful, as most agents in the role of second would be.

Could it be that Durrie had hit rock bottom and was finally ready to turn his life around?

Dear God, Quinn hoped so.

For Durrie's sake, and even more so, for Orlando's.

Whatever the reason for the change, it boded well for the job.

Quinn sat down on the bed and made a few calls, confirming arrangements he'd set up prior to leaving Los Angeles. Then he contacted Peter.

The head of the Office answered with a heartwarming "Well?"

"Everything's on track," Quinn said. "Arrived in Rio about an hour ago and have checked into the hotel."

"Good. Juarez wants to move your meeting tomorrow up to eight a.m."

"We can do eight. Location?"

"I'll have him text you the address."

"Thanks." As Quinn said this, his phone buzzed with a text, presumably from Durrie with the address where he and Ortega were eating.

"I've been thinking," Peter said. "You might want to go alone."

"Isn't it a full mission meeting?"

"It is, but…Juarez had to make a last-minute substitution on the ops team. An agent named Terrance Sala. You know him?"

"I've worked with him a couple times." Sala was a solid operative. Quinn couldn't imagine a reason why his presence would be an issue.

"Sala was on the Resnick job with Durrie last summer."

Quinn groaned inwardly. That was the gig on which the civilians at the bus stop had died. "Let me guess. No one knows Durrie's working with me."

"Of course they don't. If they did, they would have protested. So, it would probably be better if those who don't need to know remained in the dark."

No kidding, Quinn thought. The good thing was that other than the meeting tomorrow morning, there were no other instances when the ops team and the clean team would cross paths.

"No problem. I'll go to the meeting by myself," he said. "Any other fun facts I should know about?"

"Only that there are a lot of eyes on this, so don't screw it up."

"Not planning on it. Listen, um, Durrie was wondering what his next steps are after this job."

"He shouldn't be wondering about anything right now. He should be focusing on the job at hand."

"He is," Quinn said. "I just thought it might be motivation, knowing that the next thing was out there. You know, like this job was. I was thinking maybe I could mention that San Francisco job."

"San Francisco? I'm not so sure about that. I'd be much more comfortable if we kept him on things out of the country for a while." He paused. "Look, if you feel dangling something in front of him will help, that's your call. Do what you think is best."

"Thanks, Peter."

After hanging up, Quinn checked his messages and saw he'd received not one text, but two. The first was the expected message from Durrie, giving him the name of a restaurant two blocks south of the hotel. The second was from Orlando.

> Just checking in. Hope you guys had a good flight.

Though she didn't come out and ask, Quinn knew she was wondering whether or not Durrie was behaving.

He punched in a response.

> All good here.

She sent him a smiley face.

He almost put his phone away, but tapped out a second text.

> Don't worry. Everything is going to be fine.

His finger hesitated over the send arrow. The message was a violation of one of the rules Durrie had taught him. "Never promise anyone anything in this business," Quinn's mentor had said. "You're not God. You can't predict the future. And as much as you might think you know what will happen, you don't. The only thing a promise will ever get you is in trouble."

He pressed the arrow and the message was sent.

A few seconds later, Orlando replied:

Thank you.

Durrie kept the smile on his face until he exited the hotel room and Ortega had shut the door behind them.

Ortega opened his mouth to say something as they walked down the hallway, but Durrie signaled him to wait. He was positive Peter had the place bugged, so they rode the elevator down in silence.

When they reached the street, Durrie pulled a scrambler out of his pocket and flicked it on. About the size of a trio of sugar packets stacked together, the device created a sound bubble around them, preventing any microphones from picking up anything they said. It would also disrupt the transmission of any bugs Quinn might have planted on them.

Durrie was pretty sure he was clean. The only time he'd touched Quinn was when they shook hands at the airport, and since then he had meticulously avoided getting any closer than a meter to his apprentice. He hadn't even slept on the plane, only rested his eyes while keeping his senses on alert. He was less convinced Ortega hadn't been tagged. The kid was smart, but he was still learning the game.

"Okay, we can talk," Durrie said. "Thoughts?"

"He's exactly like you said he'd be."

Durrie nodded. "On the outside."

"Yeah. If you hadn't told me it's all an act, I would have never believed it."

"Johnny's one of the best. He even fooled me before. You gotta stay on your toes, Angel. Behind that calm expression hides the mind of someone who'd prefer I was out of the picture."

"And after all you did for him. What an asshole."

Durrie nodded again but said nothing this time.

"I guess this means your plan is a go."

A snort from Durrie. "I wish I had another choice."

"Don't worry. You know you can count on me."

Durrie smiled and clapped Ortega on the back. "I do."

Quinn joined Durrie and Ortega at the restaurant before their meals were served, and he and his old mentor ended up telling stories to Ortega from when Quinn was an apprentice.

While a few glasses of wine helped lubricate the conversation, it was Durrie's willingness to open up and talk about things that didn't always put himself in the best of light that convinced Quinn to share tidbits he would have normally kept to himself.

It reminded Quinn of the times during his apprenticeship when Durrie would take him along to evenings out with other members of a team. Quinn would sit and listen to their tales and the boasts, soaking up every moment of it. That was probably how Ortega was feeling now, and a part of Quinn couldn't help but feel a little envious of the kid.

As they walked back to the hotel, Quinn touched Durrie on the arm, slowing him so that Ortega moved ahead of them.

In a low voice, Quinn said, "I looked into my schedule, and there's something coming up next week that I might be able to use you on."

"Really?" Durrie said, appearing surprised. "That's great news. Where is it?"

Quinn hesitated. He'd been planning on just dropping the info about a possible job without going into details. But as Peter had said, it was his call, and he thought telling Durrie might help improve his performance. "It's…in San Francisco."

"That would be fantastic."

"It will still depend on how things go here, of course."

"Sure."

"And I'll need to clear it with Peter."

"Of course."

"But I don't see any reason why it won't happen."

Durrie grinned. "Thanks, Johnny."

An hour later, Durrie lay in his bed, staring at the ceiling.

San Francisco.

He snorted.

Yeah, he knew what that job was.

Quinn, what a two-faced bastard.

Durrie had asked the question about another job as a test. He always figured Peter and Quinn's plan was to have the Rio job go smooth as silk, then follow it up with the mission on which they would terminate him. He knew Quinn had been lying on the plane when he said he'd have to look into his schedule. The asshole had known from the beginning what was next. He just wanted to make the offer look natural.

Durrie had to give him credit. If he hadn't been on to Quinn's game from the start, Durrie would have bought the lie. But since he was in the know, when Quinn mentioned something was coming up, Durrie had had to fight to keep the sneer off his face. And when his apprentice said it would take place in San Francisco, that sealed the deal.

A US location, at a port city, where there would be plenty of agency backup if necessary. An obvious choice for the removal of someone they had labeled redundant.

Too bad for them things didn't always go as planned.

18

E nrique Juarez opened the door and smiled at Quinn. "There
he is. Good to see you, buddy." The man pulled Quinn into
a bear hug before letting him inside and looking past him into the
hallway. "You alone?"

"Had some errands I needed my guys to take care of this
morning. I'll fill them in on anything they need to know later."

Quinn had tasked Durrie and Ortega with scoping out their
route, from the warehouse in which the termination would occur
to the mortuary that was the backup body disposal site, as well as
checking out the mortuary itself. To Quinn's relief, Durrie and
Ortega had taken to the task without questioning why they
weren't included in the op meeting.

Juarez led Quinn over to the table where the rest of his strike
team was gathered.

Motioning to each of the others in turn, the op leader said,
"Gary Crist, Hannah Upland, Dominic Aquino, Choi Do-won,
and Terrance Sala."

Quinn shook with each of them. Crist and Aquino were new to
him, the others he'd worked with on at least one job.

Juarez got right down to it. The latest intel indicated El-Baz
was still on track to arrive the next evening. "We have satellites

watching the Saudi airfield we believe he'll be leaving from. That will be happening late tonight, our time. The satellites should also give us an exact count of how many others are traveling with him." Juarez tapped some keys and a map focused on Africa and South America appeared on the large monitor at the end of the table. "Given the type of aircraft available to him, the distance between there and here is too far to go in one shot, so he'll have to refuel on the way. Our source says that should happen here." He pointed at a spot along the west coast of the lower half of Africa. "It's a private airfield just outside of Kinshasa in the DRC." Democratic Republic of Congo. "There will be a team in place to observe them from the ground, and another satellite watching from above, to make sure anyone who gets off the plane gets back on.

"From there, it's a long trip across the South Atlantic to here." He tapped a few keys on his computer, and the map zoomed in on an airfield, near the opening of Guanabara Bay, with the initials SDU hovering above it. "Santos Dumont Airport. It's pretty much exclusively for domestic use, which means El-Baz's jet will likely be representing itself as coming from somewhere else in the country."

Using this tactic would avoid the scrutiny that would come if they arrived at Galeão International Airport twenty kilometers away.

Juarez enlarged the map even more, focusing on the airport itself, and switched to a satellite image. "Okay, let's talk end of the mission first. We don't know exactly where the plane will be parked, but our best guess is one of these three locations."

With a touch of a key, three arrows appeared on the map, two at points along the building just north of the commercial terminal, and one near a building at the southern end of the airfield.

Juarez looked at Quinn. "Whichever it is, you'll bring the cargo in through this gate." Another arrow appeared at one of the airport's gated entrances. The ops leader picked up a packet from the table and tossed it to Quinn. "ID badges for you and your team. You just need to insert pictures. There's also a sticker that needs to be put on your vehicle. You'll be on the list of expected deliveries so there shouldn't be any problems." He paused. "One of you speak Portuguese, right?"

"I do," Quinn said. Ortega apparently did, too, but there was no need to mention that.

"Great." Juarez nodded across the table at two members of his team. "Hannah and Dominic should have the remote controls installed by the time you arrive. If you need the assistance, they can help transfer the bodies."

Quinn nodded. Since Sala wouldn't be there, Quinn didn't need to say no to having the extra hands available.

"Once you're done," Juarez continued, "you'll exit the way you arrived, then proceed to the standby location here." The spot was a small parking lot about a dozen blocks away. "Hannah and Dominic will handle things from there."

Hannah nodded. "As soon as the plane is closed up and Quinn has left the airport, we will radio for takeoff clearance. Dominic and I will remotely fly the plane to the crash zone over the Atlantic, where we will ditch it."

Juarez said to Quinn, "Once the plane is airborne, you're released."

If something happened that prevented the plane from leaving —problems with the remote control or issues with getting clearance in a timely manner—Quinn's team would return, pick up the bodies, and use the mortuary to dispose of El-Baz and his men. Hopefully it wouldn't come to that.

"So, that's the easy part," Juarez said with a grin. "Let's talk about the takedown."

Over the next twenty minutes, Juarez went step by step through the plan to ensnare El-Baz and eliminate him and his bodyguards. Juarez went through all the ways things could go wrong, and the contingencies his team would enact for each.

It was all good information for Quinn, but his team's only

responsibility during this stage would be getting into position to deal with the aftermath.

By the time the meeting ended, it was nearly 9:45 a.m.

"I'll let you know as soon as we have confirmation that the plane had left Saudi Arabia," Juarez said as he walked Quinn to the door.

"Thanks," Quinn said, then shook Juarez's hand again. "Good luck."

Quinn spent the rest of the morning doing drive-bys of the airport and the takedown location, a few kilometers northwest of SDU at the Port of Rio. He'd picked out several routes between the two places during his prep time in L.A., and now that he was in country, he was able to drive and rank them from most to least desirable. He also identified shortcuts between the routes, in case situations arose that forced his team to improvise. As Durrie had taught him early on, preparation was key to every successful mission.

At one p.m. he met up with Durrie and Ortega for lunch, at a small restaurant a few blocks from Ipanema Beach. After filling them in on the ops meeting, he said, "How did your visit go?"

"The route is easy enough. But I gotta say, given the number of bodies we're talking about, the mortuary isn't as big a place as I would like," Durrie said. "It'll take him a couple days to get through everyone."

"That's not ideal," Quinn agreed.

"Are there any other places we can use?" Ortega asked. "You know, spread the load?"

"This was the only crematorium I found that would service our needs," Quinn said. "But maybe Peter has some contacts I'm unaware of. I'll check with him."

"He's bound to know someone," Durrie said. "But here's to

everything going smoothly so we don't have to worry about alternatives."

It was a surprisingly upbeat outlook. Even on-top-of-his-game Durrie from back in the day would seldom say anything so rosy.

After lunch, they picked up the remaining items they needed, including the cargo van they would be using the next day. Quinn then showed them the routes he'd chosen between the termination site and the airport. By the time they arrived back at the hotel, the sun had set.

Durrie and Ortega went out to dinner together again. This time when asked if he wanted to join them, Quinn begged off. He wanted to spend a few hours studying everything again, making sure he hadn't missed any details.

Instead of heading straight to dinner, Durrie and Ortega ran a few errands of their own first.

19

"Hey, babe."

Orlando smiled at the sound of Durrie's voice. "Hi. I didn't think I was going to hear from you."

"Had a little time. Thought I'd see how things were going there."

"Quietly. Just reading a book." The hardback lay on the couch beside her, opened to the same page she'd been trying to get through for the last hour. Her mind kept drifting to thoughts about Durrie and Quinn's mission. "How are you doing?"

"Fine. I mean, it's Rio, right? Nothing to complain about."

"You eat dinner yet?" Though it was barely five p.m. in San Diego, it was nine p.m. in Rio.

"Just finished."

"Good. I was thinking about scrounging up something myself."

He said nothing for a second, then, "We'll know if we're a go by the morning."

Telling her this was a breach of protocol. Mission particulars were not to be shared with anyone not directly involved, especially this close to actual engagement time. But she was glad he did.

"Everything look good?" she asked.

"Yeah. Solid plan. Plenty of contingencies."

"Happy to hear it." When he didn't say anything, she said, "You'll call me when you're done?"

"If you want me to."

"Of course I do."

"Then I'll call."

"I love you," she said.

"Love you, too. I'll, um, I'll talk to you soon."

The line went dead.

She lowered the phone into her lap and stared at it.

"It's fine," she whispered. "It's all going to be fine."

Quinn looked up from his computer and rolled his head over his shoulders. His stomach growled so he checked the time—9:47 p.m. He'd been at it for over two and a half hours.

He stood and stretched, then listened at the door to Durrie and Ortega's room. Hearing nothing, he knocked. When no one answered, he considered opening the door and taking a look but thought better of it. They were probably still out, grabbing a drink somewhere and relaxing before the big day. Quinn couldn't help feeling a bit worried that Durrie might overindulge, but his mentor had behaved well so far. Hopefully, it would be fine.

Quinn's stomach growled again.

He left his room and went down to the ground floor, thinking he'd grab a quick bite to eat at the place where they'd had dinner the night before. As he was nearing the lobby's exit, Durrie and Ortega walked in. Neither looked inebriated, though they did appear surprised to find him there.

"Something up?" Durrie asked.

"Just got hungry," Quinn replied.

"You should have joined us. We found a place about a half

kilometer from here that had great *feijoada*. I can tell you how to get there if you want."

"That's all right. I'm going to get something down the block."

"Your loss. Think I'll go up and hit the sack."

"Me, too," Ortega said.

"Sleep well," Quinn said. "See you in the morning."

They headed to the elevator and Quinn went outside, glad his concern about Durrie's drinking had proven untrue.

He had the sudden urge to call Orlando and give her another update on Durrie. He even went so far as to slip his hand into his pocket, but he let go of his phone before he could pull it out, knowing the real reason he'd be calling was to hear her voice.

And that would be disrespectful to both her *and* Durrie. Granted, neither would ever suspect the actual reason behind his call, but Quinn would know and that was enough.

He ate quickly and returned to the hotel. The door between his and the others' room was closed and all was quiet. He sat down at the desk and started going over the plans again. At 11:06 p.m. Juarez sent him a text.

El-Baz is airborne. Seven others in his group, plus two pilots.

Unless the plane headed somewhere unexpected, it appeared the mission was officially on.

Durrie stopped talking the moment he heard the door to Quinn's room open. He moved quietly over to their shared doorway, and listened as Quinn walked through his room. A squeak of what sounded like a chair being moved, and afterward only the occasional clicks from a keyboard.

Durrie returned to his bed, sat down, and whispered to Ortega, "Run through it one more time."

"Don't worry. I've got it."

"Do it."

"Okay, okay. I drive us to the port and park. You and Quinn exit and head to the building where you're supposed to wait. As soon as you're out of sight, I send the text, then I get out."

"Keep going," Durrie said.

Ortega took a breath and continued until Durrie was satisfied.

20

At ten a.m. local time—six a.m. in Rio—the freelance watchers observing the private airfield just outside Kinshasa sent a text to the team in Rio.

The Falcon has landed

They monitored the aircraft as it taxied to the small hangar at the side of the landing strip, where it was met by a fuel truck. As service to the plane began, El-Baz and his men exited and boarded two waiting Range Rovers. The SUVs then headed down the only road leading away from the field.

After a nod from Watcher 1, Watcher 2 hurried over to the pair of motorcycles they'd arrived on, climbed on his bike, and took off in pursuit of the SUVs.

Watcher 2 followed the Range Rovers at a safe distance. Not surprisingly, the SUVs headed toward the city, allowing Watcher 2 to gradually decrease the gap between them. Before long he was only a handful of car lengths away.

As the city closed in around them, the SUVs stuck to the main road for about fifteen minutes before turning into a rundown neighborhood. There, the vehicles turned every few blocks, making them trickier to follow. If not for the fact the Range Rovers hadn't increased their speed, the watcher would have wondered if he had been spotted and the serpentine path was a ploy to lose him. Even then, he couldn't help but check over his shoulder a few times to make sure a third vehicle wasn't sneaking up behind him.

Deep into the new neighborhood, the SUVs finally stopped in front of a row of shops, several of which had yet to open for the day. Each shop had painted its storefront a different color—purple or red or yellow or green or blue.

A passenger door on the front SUV opened, and one of El-Baz's people stepped out and entered an orange-fronted shop with a sign in the window reading PÂTISSERIES DE KETIA. The man remained inside for nearly two minutes before opening the door again and waving once at the SUVs. The remaining men, including El-Baz, piled out and entered the bakery.

While it was possible El-Baz just happened to be a fan of the shop's *pain au chocolat*, the watcher was no idiot and had no doubt something more sinister was going down inside.

He reported what he'd witnessed back to Watcher 1, then sent his partner a picture of the location to be forwarded to the powers that be. They undoubtedly would want to give the business a closer look.

The meeting lasted over an hour. By the time the SUVs returned to the airfield—with the watcher still following—it was ten minutes past noon.

"Anything else interesting come up?" Watcher 1 asked.

Watcher 2 shook his head. "Just a straight trip back here."

At the airfield, El-Baz's group reboarded the aircraft and the plane taxied to the end of the runway. As soon as the jet was in the air, Watcher 1 fired off another next.

The Falcon wheels up. Good luck.

USA

Fifteen minutes later, a second text went out. This one from an analyst working at the NSA Black Box outside Washington, DC.

Satellite confirmation. Jet on a west-southwest heading over Atlantic, on course for Rio.

21

RIO DE JANEIRO

Quinn donned a light blue windbreaker and zipped it closed, covering most of the black, long sleeve T-shirt he wore underneath. Over his black jeans, he pulled on gray sweatpants, then slipped into a pair of off-white Converse high tops. Finally, he pulled on a New York Yankees baseball cap and a pair of black, thick-framed glasses.

He checked himself in the mirror and nodded, satisfied. It wasn't the best disguise he'd ever worn, but that wasn't the point of the outfit. Its job was merely to ensure that, if things went awry, no one would report seeing anyone wearing all black leaving the building.

He grabbed his small duffel off the bed and knocked on the adjoining door.

"It's unlocked," Ortega called.

Quinn opened the door and stepped into the room shared by the rest of his team. Ortega was standing near the window, dressed in a similar fashion to Quinn.

Quinn raised an eyebrow, silently asking about Durrie.

Ortega nodded his chin toward the bathroom. Seconds later, the sound of a flushing toilet was followed by running water and Durrie exiting.

"Sorry," he said. "Angel was hogging the bathroom earlier."

"No worries," Quinn said. "Everyone ready?"

"Hell, yeah," Ortega replied.

"Let's do this," Durrie said.

Quinn handed out the comm gear. Once they all had their earpieces on, he led his team down to the lobby.

"You're up," Quinn said to Ortega.

Ortega grinned and headed out the front door, while Quinn and Durrie followed at a more leisurely pace. By the time the two cleaners reached the sidewalk, Ortega was halfway down the block, walking at a brisk—though not attention-gaining—pace.

Quinn glanced at Durrie. His mentor was staring ahead, as if he had something on his mind.

"You okay?" Quinn asked.

There was the slightest of delays before Durrie looked over and smiled. "I'm good, Johnny. Don't worry. You can count on me."

"I know I can," Quinn said, believing Durrie's words more than he would have two days earlier.

A click came over the comm, followed by, "Ortega for Quinn."

"Go for Quinn."

Ortega was out of sight, having made a left turn at the upcoming intersection.

"Area looks clear. I'm proceeding to the van."

"Copy."

When Quinn and Durrie reached the corner, they paused and turned to each other, just a couple of friends stopping mid-walk in conversation.

"If you've got any questions," Quinn said in a low voice, "now is as good a time as any to ask."

Durrie shook his head. "Like I said, Johnny, you don't have to worry about me. I'm as ready as I've ever been."

Quinn wasn't so sure about that. Back in the day, no one knew the ins and outs of a job better than Durrie. But that said, Durrie *had* put in a good amount of prep work on this one. When they went over the plan one last time that morning, Durrie had all but led the session, reciting the smallest detail from memory.

"After we finish, I'll talk to Peter about that San Francisco job," Quinn said. "As long as you're still interested."

Durrie grinned. "Thanks. I'd really appreciate it."

"I'm always here for you. Whatever you need. I hope you know that."

"Oh, I do, Johnny. You are nothing if not reliable."

That wasn't exactly the response Quinn was expecting, but before he could think about it too much, the comm crackled to life again.

"Ortega for Quinn."

"Go for Quinn."

"Van's clear. Come on down."

They headed to the port, Ortega behind the wheel, Quinn in the front passenger seat, and Durrie crouched in the space between them. In the back of the van were the two crates containing cleaning supplies and body bags that had arrived with them on the plane.

The bags would be a temporary measure, of course, meant only to aid in transporting the dead from the scene of the takedown to the plane. Once the team transferred them to the jet, the dead men would be unwrapped and strapped into the seats.

As for the cleaning solutions, if everything went the way Juarez planned, Quinn and his team wouldn't have to crack open any but the mildest of solvents. The gas Juarez was going to use was odorless and invisible, and should quickly render El-Baz and his men unconscious. The ops team would then administer a lethal dose of Beta-Somnol beneath a toenail of each terrorist, theoretically finishing the job without a drop of blood being spilt. The only cleanup would be removing any fingerprints and hairs left behind by the victims and ops team.

The long shadows of the late afternoon hung over the streets, causing the brake lights in the horrendous traffic to shine all the brighter.

Quinn checked his watch. It was 6:23 p.m. He looked out the side window, toward Santos Dumont Airport, as if he might be able to pick out El-Baz's jet on final approach.

The traffic signal ahead changed to yellow. Ortega gunned the engine, rushing the van into the intersection a split second before the light turned red. The cars ahead of him, though, were at a dead stop, leaving him only enough room to get the front half of the van out of the intersection.

A traffic cop, who'd been standing at the corner, strode into the road, blowing repeatedly on his whistle and motioning for Ortega to pull forward. But until everyone else started moving, the van wasn't going anywhere.

The cop continued toward them, his whistle working overtime. It wasn't until he was a few meters away that he dropped the device from his lips and began yelling at them in Portuguese. Before he reached their vehicle, though, the line of traffic moved.

Quinn watched the cop out of the side of his eye. For a moment, it looked as if the officer would still pursue them, probably to give them a ticket, but then he turned away as something else grabbed his attention.

As soon as Quinn was sure they were safe, he turned to Ortega.

Before he could say anything, Durrie spoke up, his voice terse. "Don't ever do that again. If it's turning yellow, you stop."

Ortega glanced over at Durrie and then at Quinn. "Sorry."

"Don't be sorry, be smart," Durrie told him. "It's the little things that can trip you up."

Quinn almost grinned at hearing two of Durrie's favorite rules in the same breath.

"It won't happen again," Ortega said.

"That's all we can ask."

While the smackdown had been vintage Durrie, it had ended

in an uncharacteristically forgiving way. Quinn could not recall a single time Durrie had ever let him off the hook that easily back in his apprentice days.

When they were a couple of blocks from the warehouse where the operation would occur, Quinn received a text from Juarez.

Touchdown

El-Baz looked out the window as his jet taxied toward a hangar north of the passenger terminal. He had never been to South America. It was a continent full of heretical Catholics, with few fellow Muslims to be found. The day would come, of course, when that would change, but he would leave that to others. He was more concerned about ridding the home of Islam of its Western influences. And *that* was the only reason for this trip. Tonight, he would be meeting with an arms merchant named Varela, to close a deal that would keep El-Baz's organizations equipped with gear and ammunition for years to come.

When the plane finally stopped, Omar Urabi, El-Baz's chief of security, was the first off. The Falcon watched as Urabi and several members of the security detail thoroughly examined the waiting SUVs for bombs and tracking bugs.

Upon his return, Urabi announced, "The vehicles are ready."

El-Baz stood and followed his protector down the stairs to the tarmac.

The plan to take down El-Baz was hatched within a day after the source inside El-Baz's organization informed his handlers in Washington about the meeting with Varela.

The trick had been to arrange for Juarez instead of the arms dealer to be waiting for El-Baz at the meet location. This entailed a separate strike team intercepting Varela before he arrived at the site, and making sure he and his men had no chance to warn the Falcon.

As El-Baz's aircraft was making its final approach to Santos Dumont Airport, Varela, his two advisors, and his four-man security detail exited the Belmond Copacabana Palace Hotel through a side exit and hurried into a waiting van. When the vehicle pulled away from the hotel, a sedan containing two members of team Omega—the Varela strike team—followed. Two other Omega sedans kept pace with Varela's vehicle, on the streets to either side.

Seventeen minutes later, at approximately the same time El-Baz's jet was taxiing to the hangar, Omega's team leader radioed, "Omega Prime to Decoy Three."

"Go for Decoy Three."

"Target continuing on route Blue. Looks like you're the winner." The strike team had five separate decoy teams set up, covering all of Varela's likely routes.

"Copy. Decoy Three ready."

Pursuit continued for several minutes before Prime said, "Decoy Three, two minutes out."

"Copy, Omega Prime."

"Pursuit, reconfigure."

"Copy. Omega Two moving into point position," the agent in one of the other sedans said.

"Omega Three, flanking." This from the third sedan.

The intersection was only a kilometer from the port and had been chosen because of the large construction project in the area. Though work routinely continued until late in the night, on this evening, the construction personnel had been given a rare day off. This had been arranged thanks to a "problem" discovered during an inspection that morning.

The area was lit up like it was still in operation, but the only workers present were the two members of Decoy Three, one sitting in the driver's seat of a faded yellow earthmover, and the other standing nearby, holding a perforated metal pole with a stop sign reading *PARE* attached to the top. If one took a long look at the sign, he or she would notice it was not the normal shape, and instead looked more like a custom shade for a car window. It was, however, painted in a way to make that less obvious, something also helped by the twilight.

"Thirty seconds," Omega Prime said.

The man with the sign looked down the road, searching for the van. The moment he saw it, he signaled his partner on the earth-mover and stepped toward the road, affecting the persona of a bored construction worker nearing the end of a long day. He waved cars past him until there was only the sedan containing Omega Two between him and the van. He raised his free hand in the universal gesture for halt and turned the sign so that the drivers of the sedan and the van could read it. Both vehicles slowed to a stop. A moment later, Omega Prime and Omega Three halted behind the van. The sign holder signaled to the earthmover that the road was clear.

The construction vehicle rolled onto the asphalt, and lurched to a stop as its engine abruptly quit. The driver played with the controls as if trying to get the vehicle going again, then acted confused when the tractor "refused" to move.

In perfect Brazilian Portuguese, the sign holder shouted, "What's wrong?"

The driver, also selected for his language skills, called back, "Something popped. I think it's the shaft again." He climbed off his seat, dropped to the ground, and leaned down to inspect the underside of his vehicle.

Looking exasperated, the sign holder walked up to the sedan at the front of the line.

"Sorry," he said to the operative behind the wheel, still speaking Portuguese. "It should just be a few moments."

He proceeded to the van. The driver looked at him through the closed window, so he mimed for the guy to open it.

The driver was one of Varela's security men and seemed reluctant to do so. The faux road worker stepped right up and repeated the motion of winding down the window. Finally, the driver relented, lowering the glass halfway.

The sign holder smiled. "I'm sorry, it's just a small technical problem." As he spoke, he turned the rod the sign was attached to, pointing the short barrel hidden inside it at the driver's shoulder. "It should only be a few minutes at most."

The man looked at him, clearly not understanding anything the agent had said. The agent smiled, then with a timing he'd been perfecting over the last twenty-four hours, he depressed the button on the rod that fired the dart, while activating the disk he held in his other hand and tossing it into the van.

The driver jerked as the dart embedded itself in his arm, but he passed out before he could make another move.

The man in the front passenger seat reached toward his jacket, going for his weapon. Unfortunately, he was closest to where the disk had landed, and thus the first to inhale the invisible, odorless gas the device secreted. He swayed sideways into the passenger-side door, blinking rapidly, then fell forward against the dash, unconscious.

The second the passenger started to sway, the agent had moved the sign so that it perfectly covered the driver's-side window. The gas quickly moved through the vehicle, incapacitating Varela and his remaining associates within seconds of their registering they were in trouble.

The sign holder waited until the last man had passed out before tossing in a second disk, which released a deactivating agent that would turn most, but not all, of the gas into harmless particles. He then walked toward Omega Prime, the car directly behind the van, as if continuing his informational trek.

The moment he started walking away from Varela's vehicle, the passenger door of Omega Two's sedan opened and the agent inside exited. The agent approached the van, slipping a small, almost unnoticeable respirator into his mouth and pulling on a pair of glasses with clear plastic side guards. He unlocked the driver's door through the still open window and opened it.

The agent disconnected the driver's seatbelt, pushed the unconscious man onto the floor, and climbed behind the wheel. After a quick visual check to make sure all of his passengers were still unconscious, he signaled the man on the earthmover.

The faux construction worker climbed back on and "tried" the engine again. This time it miraculously restarted.

The sign holder hurried back to his position and, as soon as the earthmover moved out of the way, waved the cars through.

The convoy of the three Omega cars and the Varela van proceeded to a plane waiting at Afonos Air Force Base, approximately twenty kilometers from the ambush site. From there, the now former arms dealer and his men would be flown to a black site in eastern Europe for several rounds of intense questioning.

Varela's capture was a pleasant bonus to the El-Baz operation.

A similar abduction procedure had been considered for the Falcon and his party. But the fact that the terrorist would probably be traveling with a larger group and require multiple vehicles—both of which turned out to be true—the idea was dismissed. Better to get him out of his vehicle and into the location of his meeting.

Juarez's team had studied the warehouse's plans and gone over the satellite images until each member had committed the information to memory. The only thing they had not done was physically visit the site. Though surveillance indicated the building had remained empty for the two days prior to the meeting, Juarez didn't want to chance that Varela was also having the place watched. So, the building was to remain off limits until Varela had been neutralized.

Word of the arms dealer's capture arrived at 6:48 p.m., as Juarez, Sala, Crist, and Choi sat in a sedan a few blocks away from the warehouse.

As soon as Juarez finished reading the text, he clicked on his comm mic. "Juarez for Quinn."

"Go for Quinn."

"Varela has been removed. We are officially a go."

"Copy."

Juarez looked over at Sala in the driver's seat. "Let's go."

Hannah and Dominic received a text from Juarez with the same information, as they sat in the bar of the Prodigy Hotel, which was connected directly to the passenger terminal at Santos Dumont Airport.

Dominic downed the last of his cola while Hannah set more than enough cash on the bar to cover their drinks and tip.

They rode the elevator up to the fourth floor, Dominic carrying an extra wide briefcase, and proceeded toward the rooms where the two pilots of El-Baz's jet were staying. Twenty minutes earlier, they had witnessed the men arriving. As the pilots checked in, Hannah had approached the checkout counter between them, and asked the clerk what time breakfast would be served the next morning. As the clerk answered, Hannah adhered tiny tracking disks to the bottom of each pilot's suit coat.

She had returned to the bar, where she and Dominic monitored the pilots on a handheld tracking device as the men went up to their rooms. One of the disks had continued to move around its pilot's room the entire time. The other, however, had become stationary within a minute after that pilot entered his room, meaning the man had probably removed his jacket. The two agents had been keeping an eye on the lobby in case the latter pilot reappeared, but by the time they headed up, he hadn't.

They stopped in front of the first pilot's door, the man whose tracker had continued to move. From the briefcase, Dominic removed one of two gas canisters, and attached the wide flat nozzle to the canister's valve. Hannah removed her scarf and tucked it along the bottom of the door, leaving just enough space for the nozzle to fit.

"Here," Dominic said, handing her a mask to cover her mouth and nose.

After donning one himself, he inserted the nozzle under the door until it would move no further, and opened the valve. For the next ninety seconds, the same type of gas the Omega team had tossed into Varela's vehicle flooded into the room.

Hannah monitored the pilot's movements on her tracking device. At first, he continued to move around like before, but twenty seconds before the last of the gas escaped the cylinder, he slowed. A few seconds later, nearly in sync with the canister running dry, she and Dominic heard a thump inside the room. On the tracker, the bug had stopped moving.

Dominic pulled the nozzle out, removed it from the canister, and screwed it onto the other one. While he did this, Hannah snatched up her scarf and used an electronic lockpick to disengage the lock. Quietly, she pushed the door open until she could see the pilot lying on the floor, near one of the beds.

She gave Dominic a thumbs-up and shut the door again.

They moved to the other pilot's room. On the tracker, the bug was still in the same spot. Hannah put an ear to the door. For a few moments, she could hear nothing, then faintly, she picked up the sound of snoring.

They replayed the door trick with the second canister. Once it had delivered its contents, Hannah entered the room. The pilot was on the king-sized bed, tucked under the covers. He wasn't snoring any longer but still breathing deeply. The fact he'd gone to bed was a welcome break. It saved Hannah and Dominic some work. Plus, when he woke the next day, he would have no clue anything unusual had happened.

They left him there and went back to his buddy's room, where they stripped the man of his clothes and put him in bed.

The pilots had both been identified within minutes of the jet leaving Saudi Arabia, and before the aircraft had even been in the air for half an hour, dossiers on both men had been transmitted to Juarez's team. From this, Hannah and Dominic had learned both pilots enjoyed a few drinks when they weren't in the air.

They opened several beers and two small containers of whiskey from the minibar—the drinks of choice of the pilot in this room. The contents they mostly poured down the drain, but they left a little in one of the glasses, splashed some on the counter, and sprinkled the remainder on the man's clothes and face.

The nice thing about this particular gas was that it had the tendency to fog one's memory. So while the pilot wouldn't recall drinking and getting into bed, the evidence would convince him that's what had happened.

Hannah and Dominic left the hotel and made their way into the airport terminal. Using badges obtained via Peter, they entered the employees-only section and worked their way to a storeroom near an employee exit to the airfield. They changed into plane-maintenance uniforms they had stashed there earlier, and proceeded outside where an electric cart waited for them.

Driving through the area like they'd worked at SDU for years, they made their way to the jet El-Baz had arrived in and let themselves on board.

Hannah stood watch while Dominic installed the remote control gear, but it was unnecessary. No one came over to see what they were doing. Once he was done, she sent Juarez a text.

Plane is ready.

She and Dominic left the same way they came, then, out of their uniforms, retreated to a bar in the terminal, where they planned to wait until they received word the bodies were on the way.

22

The clean team's van sat in an empty parking lot near the op location, with Quinn, Durrie, and Ortega inside. Five minutes earlier, word had reached Quinn of Varela's removal from the equation. If all was going according to plan, that meant Juarez and his team were in position for El-Baz's arrival.

A little known fact of the secret world: everything wasn't always secret meetings and gunfights and body removals. In fact, the majority of a field agent's time was spent waiting.

Quinn certainly hadn't anticipated that aspect of the job when he'd accepted Durrie's offer of an apprenticeship. He'd been antsy to get to work, and had spent a lot of those early months fidgeting and thinking, *Come on, come on, come on,* as he and Durrie waited in a van or an out-of-the way room for the signal that they could start.

"You want to die young?" Durrie had asked him once.

"What? No. Why would you say that?"

They'd been in New York City, sitting in an unused apartment, their backs against the wall and their butts on the floor, waiting for the call that would spring them into action.

"Just chill out, all right?"

"I *am* chilled out."

A snort and a dismissive shake of the head. "I can hear your heart beating a mile a second from here."

Quinn grimaced and rolled his eyes.

"And then there's that," Durrie said, looking at the floor in front of Quinn.

Following his mentor's gaze, Quinn saw his own right foot rapidly bobbing up and down. He forced it to stop.

"You keep wasting all that energy," Durrie said, "someday you'll miss something on a job that will get you killed."

"I was just…" Quinn fell silent.

The smirk on Durrie's face was replaced by a slit of a mouth under a pair of steely eyes. "You were just *what*?"

Quinn struggled for a word to finish the sentence that wouldn't get him into more trouble, but really, there was only one thing he could say that wouldn't sound ridiculous. "Nothing. I'm sorry."

Durrie stared at him for a moment and then looked across the room, his expression unchanged. "Damn right, you're sorry. Do you realize how many hours you're going to spend sitting around in rooms like this?" A brief pause. "Don't even try answering that. I'll tell you. So many that you're going to lose count before this year is up. Tattoo this in your head. Being anxious takes away focus. When you're waiting, you're resting, so that when you're working, you're all there. Get me?"

"I get you."

"Are you sure?"

Quinn had answered yes at the time, but the truth was, he didn't understand what was wrong with being a little wound up.

Over the following months, however, as he participated in more and more jobs, he began to appreciate what Durrie had meant. And in the years since, he'd worked hard at perfecting the art of the wait, until he had it down to a near science.

Sitting in the front passenger seat of the van now, Quinn kept his eyes closed and his breathing slow. He visualized the path El-Baz and his people would take into the warehouse, followed by the moment Juarez activated the gas that would render the terrorists unconscious. After that would come the administration of a much more merciful execution than El-Baz deserved. But dead was dead, and the man's removal from this existence would more than compensate for the lack of a more deserving method.

"Beta One for Juarez."

Quinn opened his eyes. Beta One was charged with following El-Baz.

"Go for Juarez," the ops leader said over the comm.

"Target eighteen minutes out."

"Copy, Beta One. We're ready and waiting."

"Copy."

When Beta One radioed that El-Baz was fifteen minutes out, Quinn balled his fingers into fists and extended them, then turned to the back of the van, where his two team members sat. "It's time."

The plan was, while Quinn and Durrie moved into the primary staging position, closer to the warehouse, Ortega would wait at the van, in case things went wrong and they needed to make a quick getaway.

Quinn moved through the van, opened the rear door, and stepped outside. The moment his back was to the cargo area, Durrie held up three fingers.

Ortega nodded, and Durrie hopped out after Quinn.

Alone now, Ortega removed a disposable phone from his bag. There were two texts on it, both written by Durrie, each destined for a different number. Ortega sent the first, letting the others know the countdown had begun.

He then brought up the second, and confirmed the receiving number matched the one Durrie had made him memorize.

Where Durrie had gotten the number from, Ortega had no idea. But it had become clear in the months Ortega had been working with him that even though many people were actively working against the man, Durrie still had contacts almost everywhere.

Ortega stuck his hand in his bag again, this time removing the palm-sized sap he and Durrie had picked up on their errand run.

He took a breath. He couldn't deny being a little nervous, but there was no turning back now. And besides, Durrie had been unfairly targeted, so what Ortega was about to do was the right call.

He checked his watch. Ninety seconds left.

After placing the phone in his pocket, he quietly opened the door and slipped outside, then headed in the same direction as the other two.

Quinn and Durrie passed the first of the two buildings between them and the ops location.

As anticipated, the area was deserted. The collection of half a dozen warehouses had sat empty for over a year, as the estate of the deceased owner continued to be argued in court. Normally, two security guards would be working the property, but Varela had conveniently fixed things so that no one was here tonight.

Quinn sneaked up to the door of the next building. Though each structure was equipped with an alarm, Juarez's tech man, Dominic, had hacked into the system earlier that afternoon and disabled all the alarms.

Quinn picked the lock, opened the door, and smiled at the blessed silence that greeted him.

Ortega stopped behind the cover of a couple of old barrels. Ahead, he could see Quinn crouching in front of the door to the warehouse.

Ortega checked the time and pulled out the disposable phone.

Five.

Four.

Three.

Two.

One.

He pressed SEND.

Durrie glanced at his watch and felt a sense of gratification. His three-minute countdown had just expired, meaning he'd timed things perfectly. His hand unconsciously touched one of the pouches under his shirt, the one that sat at the base of his ribs.

A second after Quinn opened the door, Durrie put a hand on his apprentice's shoulder. "I got this."

He pushed past Quinn and hurried into the dark warehouse.

"Hey, slow down," Quinn said. "We need to make sure this place is clear first."

Durrie kept going.

Omar Urabi, in the front passenger seat of the lead SUV, scanned the road. He made no judgments about the people he saw. He was focused only on picking out anyone who might be a threat to El-Baz's safety.

When his phone beeped, he pulled it out, thinking it was a text from either El-Baz in the trailing vehicle or from his second in command back at their training camp in Pakistan. The text, however, was from a blocked number.

Abort your meeting with Varela. He has been arrested, and the Americans are waiting at the warehouse to kill you. Do not return to your aircraft. Hide and find some other way out of the country.

A concerned friend.

"Stop!" Urabi yelled.

As the driver hit the brakes, Urabi called El-Baz.

"What's going on?" El-Baz said. "Why have we stopped?"

Urabi told him about the text.

Cars honked at the two SUVs now blocking the road.

"Do you think it's true?" El-Baz asked.

"I don't know. But I do think it is better to be safe and reschedule."

A beat. "Stay on the line. I'm going to call Varela and I will conference you in so you can listen."

A couple of moments later, the sound of Varela's line ringing came through Urabi's speaker.

"Yes?" a male voice said.

"Who am I speaking to?" El-Baz said.

"It that you, Fawar? It's Matis. Matis Varela. Are you running late?"

A pause so short, Urabi was sure he was the only one who noticed. "Yes, about ten minutes at most."

"No problem. I'll be here."

"I will see you soon."

Varela was disconnected.

"Was it him?" Urabi asked.

"I'm not sure."

"Then we need to get out of here."

A pause not much longer than the last. "Yes. Do it."

Beta One was five cars back when El-Baz's SUVs came to a sudden stop. The cars behind the Range Rovers waited only seconds before starting to pull around them, several of the drivers honking as they did.

There was nowhere for Beta One to pull over, so he was forced to also go around the Range Rovers. He found an open spot about thirty meters ahead and dived into it, then watched the SUVs through his rearview mirror.

The man in the front passenger seat of the lead vehicle was talking on his phone. But why would they stop to take a phone call? Beta One clicked on his mic, and was about to report in when the man he'd been watching lowered his phone and said something to the driver.

Both SUVs pulled U-turns, garnering the scorn of drivers not just on their side of the road but also on the other, and raced off in the opposite direction.

Beta One had to wait a few seconds for an opening before he could do the same.

"Beta One for Juarez!"

"Go for Juarez."

"Something's wrong. They've just turned around and are going back the other way. Fast."

"Did they see you?"

"No. I don't think so." He explained what he'd witnessed.

"Do you still have them in sight?"

"Barely," Beta One said, his eyes on the roof of the trailing SUV a block ahead.

"Don't lose them. We need to know where they go."

"Copy."

"I got this," Durrie said, then whipped around Quinn and hurried into the building.

What the hell? Quinn thought.

"Hey, slow down. We need to make sure this place is clear first."

Either Durrie didn't hear him or was ignoring him, because he continued on.

"Dammit," Quinn muttered.

He stepped into the warehouse, following his mentor, scanning the room to make sure they were alone.

Over the comm came "Beta One for—"

Quinn continued forward, expecting the conversation to pick back up but the comm remained silent.

Ahead, Durrie was passing a small stack of wooden crates near the center of the room.

"Durrie, for God's sake, wait for me," Quinn said in a loud whisper.

Again, his mentor ignored his order.

"Durrie, stop right—"

Automatic gunfire rang out from the other side of the space. As Quinn dove to the floor, he looked toward Durrie to make sure his mentor reached cover. What he saw instead was Durrie's body jerking wildly from the impact of bullets.

No!

Quinn rolled behind a set of old crates and shimmied to the far end, thinking maybe he could arc around and come at the shooter —or shooters—from the side. As he started to move out from the boxes, though, the gunfire stopped, and was replaced by two sets of running feet across the concrete floor. A moment later, a door opened and closed, then silence.

Quinn stuck to his plan, and circled around until he had a view of where he was pretty sure the gunfire had come from. The spot looked deserted. Knowing he had very little time, he pressed his luck and ran over. Dozens of shells lay on the floor, but whoever had pulled the triggers of the guns that expelled them was gone.

Quinn scanned the area between the ambush spot and the door he'd heard open. There was no one there and nowhere to hide.

He rushed over to Durrie and dropped on his knees. Durrie lay on his stomach, blood soaking his clothes and pooling beneath him. Hoping he wasn't too late, Quinn put a hand on Durrie's throat and searched for a pulse but found nothing.

He sat back on his feet and stared at his dead teacher.

Orlando. How am I going to tell her?

Something scraped the floor directly behind him. In his shock, he took almost a second to turn to see what it was.

Ortega entered the warehouse a few moments after seeing Quinn move inside. ˙

Unlike him—and the ops team, for that matter—Ortega and Durrie had visited the site the night before, so Ortega knew all the nooks and crannies and hiding places.

He made it to the space Durrie had picked out for him just as the gunfire broke out. Ortega's hands shook. While the men Durrie had hired were mostly shooting blanks, there were a few narrowly targeted live rounds thrown into the mix, to cause damage to convince anyone who might check later this was a real attack.

When he peeked around the post he was hiding behind, Ortega saw Quinn had moved behind some boxes and was crawling away in the other direction.

Durrie had said there were only two possible responses Quinn would make: either he'd rush to the boxes next to where Durrie had gone down, or he'd try to flank the gunmen by swinging around the side. It appeared he had chosen the latter.

With Quinn's back to him for at least another few seconds, Ortega repositioned to a post only four meters from Durrie.

Boy, did Ortega's real boss look dead. The blood packets under his shirt had exploded perfectly. But it was the drug Durrie had self-administered as the shots rang out that would really sell it. By now, it would've slowed his heartbeat to nearly nothing, and all but stopped his lungs, putting Durrie in a state he had called a light death.

Ortega checked on Quinn. The cleaner was approaching the spot where the shooters had set up.

Hurry up, Ortega thought.

The longer Durrie stayed in his current condition, the higher chance his temp death would turn permanent.

Finally, Quinn hurried over to Durrie. The moment he started to kneel, Ortega silently stepped out and crept across the floor.

He was barely half a meter away when a bit of grit on the concrete rubbed against the bottom of his shoe.

Quinn started to look back but his reaction was too slow, and the sap in Ortega's hand was already arcing down at the back of Quinn's neck.

Quinn fell onto the floor next to Durrie, never having laid eyes on Ortega.

Ortega checked the cleaner and was pleased to see the single blow had been more than enough to knock Quinn out cold.

He dropped the sap and pulled a paperback-sized plastic box out of his pocket. Inside lay three preloaded syringes. He removed the longest one, felt along Durrie's ribs for the spot he'd been told to use, then plunged the needle in and injected him with a dose of adrenaline.

One moment, Durrie was aware of nothing. The next, he felt as if he were being yanked viciously through a tunnel barely wide enough to fit him. As consciousness returned, his body arched and he gasped for air.

"Jesus," he said, panting.

"Are you all right?" Ortega asked.

Durrie lay silent for several seconds, gathering a bit of strength. "That…depends. Where's…Quinn?"

"Right here." Ortega moved to the side.

Durrie turned his head and saw Quinn on the floor, maybe a meter away. He smiled. "So…it worked?"

"It worked."

"No problems?

"None."

Durrie looked at the ceiling again. "Then I guess I'm...fine." He took another breath. "What's happening...with El-Baz?"

"I-I don't know. The signal..."

Crap. Durrie had forgotten about the jammer he'd turned on after entering the warehouse. He pulled it out of his pocket and switched it off. The comm blared to life in his ear.

"Quinn, report!" Juarez was saying. "Where the hell are you?"

Durrie looked at Ortega, who stared back, nervous.

"Just like we practiced," Durrie said.

Ortega nodded and activated his mic. "This...this is Ortega. I, um, I'm working with Quinn."

"Where is he?"

"He's unconscious."

"What?"

"We...we were ambushed. Our third guy is dead. I've got them both in the van. I'm taking Quinn to our medical contact."

"Ambushed? Shit! Did you see them?"

Ortega glanced at Durrie, who mouthed, *Stick to the script.*

"No, I, um, tossed a smoke bomb between us so I could get my team out. Look, I know there's still work to do. After I get Quinn to the doctor, I'll, uh, come back for the bodies. I...might need a little help, though."

Durrie smiled. Ortega's tone had been the perfect blend of dedication and uncertainty.

"Negative," Juarez said. "We're aborting."

"Aborting? Were you ambushed, too?"

"No, but El-Baz has changed course. We don't know where he's going but he's definitely not coming here."

Ortega looked at Durrie, an eyebrow raised. Durrie thought for a moment, then shook his head. One of the contingencies they had practiced was for Ortega to try to draw more information out of Juarez, but that seemed unnecessary. El-Baz had clearly received the text and taken it seriously. Durrie was sure the terrorist would meld into the city, and eventually find his way back home.

Someday, if Durrie needed a favor, he'd let the man know who had saved him. At the moment, saving himself was priority.

He pushed into a sitting position, his strength returning. "Did you give him the drug?"

"Not yet."

"Well, get on it."

Ortega pulled a second syringe out of a small kit and stuck the needle into Quinn's arm, delivering a mild sedative that would keep Durrie's former apprentice unconscious for at least thirty minutes.

Ortega then retrieved the van and pulled it up to the door so they wouldn't have to move Quinn very far.

A few minutes later, they had Quinn strapped into the front passenger seat, and were heading toward their local medical contact.

Durrie crouched between the front seats and held his hand out to Ortega. "Syringes."

Ortega handed him the small kit, and Durrie removed the last unused needle.

"You ready?" Durrie asked.

"I guess."

"It's okay to be scared. He'll expect that. Just remember, if you stick to the points we worked on, you'll be fine."

"Okay."

"The hard part's behind us." He patted Ortega's shoulder. "You've done a great job. Thank you."

Ortega smiled, clearly happy he had pleased Durrie. "Glad I could help."

"Me, too. All right. Here we go."

Durrie gave Quinn the shot. It contained just enough stimulant to ease his apprentice into wakefulness. When Durrie was done, he took the needle kit into the back with him, climbed inside the body bag on the floor, and zipped himself up.

A sense of movement before anything else.

Then a drone of some kind of machinery. Everywhere—below, to the sides, front and back. It sounded as if it was coming from above, too.

It took several attempts before Quinn could pry open his eyelids. He seemed to be facing sideways, so he turned his head to be more in line with the rest of his body. Pain radiated in bolts from the back of his head. Slamming his eyes shut again, he reached back and fumbled around for the cause. At the base of his skull he discovered a knot, about the size of a tangerine, that was tender to the touch.

He opened his eyes again, only to squeeze them shut once more due to what seemed like dozens of lights shining directly at him. When he tried again, he lifted his lids slowly, letting the lights filter in through his lashes until he could see without squinting.

He was in a vehicle, the offending glare the headlights of cars and trucks in the opposite lanes. He glanced to the side. Ortega was in the driver's seat, of what Quinn realized was the van they'd been using for Operation Redeemer.

"Wha…what happened?" he asked.

Ortega jumped at the sound of Quinn's voice, then glanced over. "Oh, thank God. You're awake."

"How did I get in here?"

"I put you there."

"I-I don't understand."

Ortega nervously checked the vehicle's mirrors. "I was monitoring things on the comm when El-Baz started to run. Juarez tried to reach you but you didn't—"

"Wait. El-Baz ran?"

Ortega nodded. "His vehicles were about ten minutes away when they suddenly turned around and took off."

"He didn't show up?"

"No."

"Was anyone able to catch him?"

"Last I heard, they'd lost sight of him and don't know where he is now."

Son of a bitch. Quinn started to tilt his head back in annoyance, but his wound barked at him again. When the pain subsided enough, he said, "I remember I was next to Durrie, but nothing after that."

"Like I said, Juarez tried to reach you but you didn't answer. I decided I should go check. I found you and Durrie on the ground next to each other. I-I-I thought you were both dead until I saw that you were breathing. I carried you into the van. And…and then Durrie."

Quinn looked into the back and spotted the body bag on the floor.

Despair dropped on him like a boulder falling from a cliff. Orlando had been counting on him to make sure nothing bad happened to Durrie, and he had failed.

Durrie was dead.

He could imagine no scenario in which she would take the news well.

"Where are we going?" he asked.

"Dr. Carrillo's."

It took Quinn a second to remember Carrillo was their medical contact. His brow furrowed. "Durrie's gone. There's nothing he can do."

"Not for Durrie. For you." Ortega glanced at Quinn, then back at the road. "You can't see it but your neck is pretty bruised up. And that bump doesn't look good. Whoever hit you knew what they were doing. I wouldn't be surprised if you had a concussion, too."

Quinn was about to protest that he was fine, but that would've been a lie. And since the job was apparently a bust, it made sense to get himself checked out now.

They arrived at Carrillo's clinic fourteen minutes later. The doctor was waiting at the back door, having been alerted by a phone call Ortega had apparently made while Quinn was unconscious.

"If you don't need me to go in with you, I can, you know…" Ortega's gaze flicked to the back of the van.

Quinn was hesitant to let him deal with Durrie's body, but he had no idea how long he'd be at the doctor's office, and something *would* have to be done.

"All right," he said. "That's a good idea."

"What do you want me to do with him?" The implied question was whether or not they would transport Durrie back to the States as is.

Quinn thought for a moment. He wanted nothing more than to take Durrie's body home with them. But that was not protocol. And Durrie, at least the old Durrie, would have never tolerated Quinn violating protocol.

As painful as it was, he said, "The usual. But bring me back the ashes."

23

Quinn had ended up staying in Rio far longer than he'd expected, before Dr. Carrillo cleared him to fly. He would have ignored the medical warnings and flown home as soon as he could, but Peter had insisted he stay.

"Don't be an ass," Peter had told him. "There's nothing happening so important that you need to get back right away. Do as Carrillo says. I'll put you on medical leave."

If his injury had been only broken bones, Quinn knew Peter wouldn't have cared. Hell, if it had just been the blow to the back of his head, Peter probably would have insisted Quinn get on the next plane out. Undoubtedly, Peter's directive was driven by the fact Quinn had witnessed his mentor being gunned down. An event that would likely affect even the most hardened agents.

The night Ortega had taken Quinn to the doctor's office, Quinn had known he should call Orlando. Through the pain and Carrillo's examination, Quinn had played through his head countless ways of breaking the news to her. None were great, but he chose what he thought was the best of the bunch.

When the doctor stuck the needle in his arm, Quinn had assumed it was an antibiotic. Thirty seconds later, as his thoughts jumbled and his eyelids grew heavy, he realized it had been a sedative.

Perhaps that was best, he'd reasoned. He could use a little rest. And in a few hours, when he was clearheaded, he could talk to Orlando.

What he hadn't anticipated was the shot keeping him under until well into the following afternoon. As soon as he realized what time it was, his pulse had spiked. He knew Orlando would have been up all night wondering what had happened. He made the call but was sent immediately to voice mail. He hoped this meant she was getting some much needed rest. For a split second, he wondered if he should leave a message, but realized that would be a mistake.

He'd tried her again an hour later. And an hour after that. And again. And again. And again.

His anxiety grew exponentially with each unanswered call.

At nine p.m., Peter had rung him.

"Ah, good, you're awake. How's the head?"

"Sore."

"Yeah, well, to be expected," Peter said.

"Anything new on El-Baz?"

"At this point, our best guess is that he placed the ambush team there just in case anything went wrong. When they saw you guys show up, they realized it was a setup and informed their boss. They then tried to take you and Durrie out. In the meantime, El-Baz fled."

"Still no sign of him."

"No. I'm guessing he'll turn up in Saudi Arabia, or more likely Pakistan soon enough. We'll have to wait for another opportunity to take him out."

Quinn's jaw tensed. "When you do, I want to be on that job."

"If I can make it happen, I will."

Sensing Peter was about to hang up, Quinn said, "Have you... have you heard from Orlando? I've been trying all afternoon. Someone needs to let her—"

"I talked to her early this morning."

"Oh...okay. Um, good. And...you told her."

"I had to."

"I see. How did she take it?"

"About as badly as you'd expect."

Quinn closed his eyes. *Dammit.*

"Thanks for doing that," Quinn said. "I'll check in with her when I get home. See how she's holding up."

"You might want to give her a little time. She's working through a lot."

"Of course. Yes, you're right,"

As Quinn turned onto Orlando's street now, he wondered if eight days counted as enough time.

He parked at the curb in front of her place and glanced at the house. Closed shutters prevented him from seeing whether or not she was home.

He looked at the cardboard box on the seat beside him. Inside was the silver metal urn containing Durrie's ashes.

"It's going to be fine," he mumbled, but felt far from confident.

With a sigh, he picked up the box, climbed out of the car, and approached Orlando's front door. After another quick round of trying to psyche himself up, he pressed the doorbell.

She didn't answer.

In his mind, Quinn could see her sitting at her kitchen table, staring out the back window, oblivious to the ringing of the bell. Or maybe she was curled up on her bed, a pillow over her head, trying to block out the sounds of whoever was at the door.

He didn't want to ring again, but that wasn't an option. She was his best friend. He'd already missed being there for her when she found out. He wasn't about to abandon her as she tried to recover.

He pushed the bell again, but the house remained hushed.

He took a few steps back and tried to peek around the slats in the shutters covering the front window. But all he could see were shadows. He checked the other set of windows along the front, but what he could see was also dark.

He considered going into the backyard, but that would be a violation of her personal space. If she didn't want visitors, forcing himself on her was not the right move.

He took a room in a Marriott Courtyard Hotel about a mile away, and spent the afternoon sitting on the bed, staring at the cardboard box with the urn.

Once darkness had fallen, he trekked back to the house, parking in the same spot as before.

He knew before he exited the car that he should have stayed at the hotel. The shutters were still closed, and behind them not a single light glowed. The house just felt as if no one was home.

Still, he tried again, this time knocking instead of ringing the bell.

Dead silence from inside. The kind of silence that seemed to scream, "Go away!"

He made a third attempt at ten a.m. the next morning, and left the hotel for a fourth try at five p.m. As he turned onto her street, a chill ran up his arms. In the time between his morning visit and now, a FOR SALE sign had been planted in Orlando's front yard.

Leaving the urn in the car, he jogged up to the front door and knocked hard. "Orlando? Orlando, it's me. Quinn."

He knocked again and again, not realizing at first that the sound was creating an odd echo inside. An echo that he recognized, when it finally registered, as one that could have only been created by a room devoid of furniture.

He checked the street to make sure no one was watching him. Then, against the voice in his head saying he was making a mistake, he used his lockpicks to open the door. As he had guessed, there was nothing in the living room. He walked through the place. Every room was empty and had been cleaned.

Back in his car, he called the number on the real estate sign.

A woman answered in a cheery voice. "Becca Cox, Townside Realty."

"Yes, I'm calling about one of your listings," Quinn said, forcing himself to sound upbeat.

"Of course. Which one are you interested in?"

Quinn gave her Orlando's address.

"You're quick. That just went up on the MLS about an hour ago." She gave him the home's particulars. "We'll be holding an open house on both Saturday and Sunday if you'd like to come by."

"I'll make sure to do that." He paused. "I am curious, though. The people who lived there—I used to know them a little. Friends of friends. I know they were looking for a bigger place. I'm guessing they finally found it?"

Cox hesitated. "Actually, the boyfriend recently passed away."

"Oh, my God. I didn't know."

"It's very sad."

He almost asked where Orlando had gone but was stopped by the fact he had no idea what name she had used to buy the house. Besides, the agent probably wouldn't have told him anyway.

"I appreciate your time," he said. "I'll see you this weekend."

Back at his hotel room, he tried to break into Townside Realty's computer system but failed to get through its firewall. While he could handle hacking into a basic system—and on occasion even ones a bit more advanced—cyberespionage was not his forte. Usually when he came up against something like this, he'd call Orlando for help. Obviously, she was not an option now.

He made a few inquiries and was finally put in touch with a hacker named Jones. It took the man exactly seventy-five seconds to breach the company's security measures and provide Quinn with direct access to Townside's records. All done for the low, low price of one thousand dollars.

Quinn hunted through the system, collecting everything he could find related to Orlando's house. All of the official documents would have been done on paper. A few of these had been scanned into the computer, but as far as he was able to discover, most had not been. There were, however, over two dozen emails that gave him most of the information he was looking for.

The names she and Durrie had owned the house under were Charlotte Cullen and Edward Spanner. In an email sent three days earlier by "Charlotte" was the following:

I realize I am rushing things, listing the house so quickly, but as I'm sure you can understand, I can't stay here any longer. The movers are coming tomorrow morning, and I will have the house cleaned and ready for you by the evening. It will be best if we communicate via email, as I will be visiting friends where cell service is spotty. If you need to talk to me, send me a message and I will call you.

One day.

Quinn had missed her by one day.

He debated for nearly an hour on whether or not to send an email to the address she'd used with the realtor. Messages he'd sent to her regular email—as well as texts and calls to her phone—had gone unanswered.

It was unlikely he'd hear back from her, but he decided to try.

Orlando—

I am so sorry that I was unable to get ahold of you sooner. I know you're going through a lot. I just want you to know I'm here for you. Please, when you have a moment, contact me.

Quinn

He hit SEND.

He was right. He didn't hear back.

24

"Had a little issue with someone who was working later than she was supposed to," Quinn told Peter over the phone. "But Julien was able to distract her while I moved the body."

Julien De Coster was a French freelancer and a giant of a man. Taking advantage of the maintenance uniform he was wearing for the job, he'd removed a vacuum cleaner from a supply closet and run it in the hallway outside the woman's office. Within moments, she had shut her door. He'd continued running the machine back and forth until after Quinn had disappeared through the exit at the other end of the hall, with the bagged body over his shoulder.

"Did she see his face?" Peter asked.

"His back was to her door when she closed it, so we don't think so."

"Okay. Good. Thank you." Typically, Peter would have given Quinn a *we'll talk later* and hung up, but instead he said, "I have some information for you."

"Sure. Go ahead," Quinn said, assuming it concerned the next job.

"I know where Orlando is."

For a moment, the whole world stopped. Outside of Peter's

words echoing in his head, Quinn could hear nothing, see nothing, feel nothing.

"You still there?" Peter asked.

"Uh, yes. Yeah, I'm here. Where is she?"

"San Francisco."

San Francisco? That was just an hour-and-a-half flight away from his place in L.A.

"I have an address if you want it," Peter said.

"Can you text it to me?"

"Are you sure? Maybe it would be better if—"

"I'm sure."

A pause. "Okay."

Quinn caught a nonstop ten a.m. Delta flight to L.A. the next day. Because of the time difference from Paris, he arrived at 12:30 p.m. that same afternoon. An hour and a half later, he reached his townhouse in Studio City.

He took a quick shower, repacked his duffel bag, and grabbed the cardboard box containing Durrie's urn before returning to his car. It took him twenty minutes to reach the much closer Burbank airport. Before leaving France, he had booked tickets on two different flights to San Francisco, the second in case he missed the 3:48 p.m. flight. He did not, though he was the last to board.

The sun was low in the sky by the time he reached the street of the address Peter had given him. The neighborhood was lined with two- and three-story row houses. Several had been refurbished, but most were in need of a little TLC.

Open parking spots were scarce, and Quinn was forced to leave his rental two blocks away and one street over.

Cardboard box under his arm, he hiked back to the address. The two-story building was one of the places that could have used, at the very least, a new coat of paint. He walked up the steps to the porch, and knocked before he lost his nerve.

He heard a shout inside. A few seconds later, steps approached the door. When it opened, an elderly Asian woman looked out. She was small with a kindly face, and hair more gray than black.

"Can I help you?" she said. Her accent sounded Korean, which would make sense, given that Orlando was half.

"I'm looking for—" Orlando? That was the only name he knew her by, just like Jonathan Quinn was the only name she knew for him. But neither was the name they'd been born with. He hesitated before an idea hit him. "For Charlotte."

"And who you?"

"Quinn."

She looked him up and down, said, "You wait," and shut the door.

Barely half a minute passed before he heard steps heading back his way. When the door opened, however, it was the old woman again, not Orlando.

"She not want to see you."

The woman started to close the door.

"Wait," Quinn said.

She paused and stared at him.

"I, um, I have something for her." He glanced at the box in his hands.

"Give to me. I give to her."

"No. I…I need to give it to her personally."

The woman's eyes narrowed.

"It's important."

Frowning, she closed the door. As her steps once more retreated into the house, he wondered if no one would come back. After five minutes of silence, he was no longer wondering.

If he left, he'd have to come back tomorrow, and if necessary the day after that, and so on. He rapped on the door again.

For several moments, there was no response. Then, just as he lifted his hand for another try, he heard footsteps heading toward him.

They stopped a mere meter away, but the door remained closed.

"Go away, Quinn," Orlando said from the other side. "I don't want to see you."

"Please," Quinn said. "I just want to talk for a few minutes. That's all."

"I-I can't."

"I have something for you."

"I don't want anything from you."

Out of desperation, he said, "I promise, after we talk I'll go away and won't come back."

Silence.

"Please," he said. "Just a few minutes."

After a beat, the door creaked open. Instead of inviting him in, Orlando stepped outside and shut the door behind her.

"What do you want?" she said. She glared at him, no trace of friendship in her expression.

"I'm sorry. I can't even express how much. I should have been the one who told you."

She sneered. "You think that's why I'm angry? That you didn't *tell* me?" A shake of her head. "How I learned about…what happened doesn't matter. It's that it happened at all. That's what pisses me off."

"I swear, I'd give anything to change what happened."

"You were *there*. You should have protected him. Now my son will never know his father."

Quinn blinked. "Did you-did you say…son? I didn't even know you were pregnant."

"Yeah? Well, neither did I."

A son. With Durrie.

Jesus.

Quinn hadn't thought he could feel even worse about Durrie's death, but he'd been wrong.

"I'm so sorry. I…I haven't been able to stop thinking about what happened. I keep running the mission through my mind, trying to figure out what I could have done differently. Believe me, I know how devastating this is. How you feel, and—"

"You what? You think you know how *I* feel? There's no way you can understand what it's like to be lying there at night, your baby crying, and no one else but you to comfort him. *Forever*. Tell me, can you *feel* what that's like?"

"No, of course not. I-I-I didn't mean—"

"Just stop talking. I don't want to hear anything else. Go back to Los Angeles."

His mouth bone dry, he said, "I brought this for you."

He opened the top of the box and started to tilt it so she could see what was inside. But she turned back to the house and pushed the door open without looking. "Leave me alone. I don't ever want to talk to you again."

One of the hardest things for Quinn to ever do was tell Orlando no, and seeing her as hurt as she was, he wasn't going to start doing so today. "Okay," he said.

She stepped inside and closed the door, emphasizing the end of their conversation—their relationship?—with the clack of the dead bolt.

He stared at the door, shaken unlike he'd ever been before. His last ounce of hope tried to convince him she'd come back out. That she would see, despite everything, he cared deeply about her and only wanted to help. But after several minutes, the door remained closed and his hope drained away completely.

He placed the box on the porch, where it wouldn't be seen from the street, and left.

Orlando sat on the floor, her back to the door of Aunt Jeong's house, tears flooding down her face.

She could sense Quinn was still on the porch, in the same spot he'd been. She knew she should go back out there. That she should tell him she was sorry.

Yes, she was angrier with him than she'd been with almost anyone ever. He'd been with Durrie. He'd known Durrie wasn't operating at a hundred percent. But Quinn wasn't the only target of her ire.

The person she was angriest with was herself.

She was the one who'd pushed Durrie to take the job, when she could see he wasn't ready. She was the one who had told Quinn everything would be all right, when she'd known that wasn't true.

She had been avoiding Quinn for months, because it allowed her to focus more on the fact that Durrie was gone than the reasons why, and kept at bay the guilt buried deep inside her. Perhaps, after another few months had gone by, after Durrie had been gone for a full year, she might've been able to come to terms with her own culpability. Which then would have allowed her to forgive and reconnect with her closest friend.

But Quinn had surprised her by showing up like this. Her anger at everything flared uncontrollably, and she had done the one thing she should have never done—focused all her ire on him.

What am I going to do?

A noise out on the porch, then the sound of Quinn finally walking away.

She stayed where she was for another minute or two, then pushed to her feet and looked out the peephole. Quinn was gone, but he'd left the box behind.

She opened the door and approached the package. He'd closed the top again, so she crouched beside it and pulled the flaps open.

Her breath caught in her throat.

Oh, God.

An urn.

Quinn had broken protocol and brought Durrie back to her.

Tears welled again, but before they could stream down her cheeks, she heard the cry of her son, Garrett, waking from his nap.

She wiped her eyes, picked up the box, and headed back inside.

"It's okay, sweetie. Mommy's coming."

From his window seat on the night flight back to L.A., Quinn stared out at the vast darkness of the Pacific Ocean.

He had failed Durrie. He had failed himself. But most of all, he had failed Orlando and her newborn son. He brooded on this for nearly half the trip, before he recalled the conversation he and Durrie had had in the parking lot at Leonetti's. He remembered something that—ironically—Durrie had once said.

Quinn had done something wrong on a job, and in the days after, had continued to beat himself up over it.

"Look, Johnny," Durrie had finally said one afternoon. "You can learn from the past, but you can't do anything to change it. The only thing you can affect is what happens next. Get me?"

If she needs anything, and I'm not there to help, you make sure she gets it.

There was nothing Quinn could do about the past. He could only affect the future. So what if Orlando didn't want to see him ever again? That didn't mean he couldn't help her and her son from afar, and in doing so, not only honor the promise he had made Durrie, but also the years of close friendship between him and Orlando.

While his mood wasn't anywhere near good, by the time he reached Los Angeles, at least he didn't feel quite as lost anymore.

EPILOGUE

Durrie stood in the living room of his sixth-floor apartment, looking through his telescope. It was aimed not at the stars above San Francisco, but at the house four blocks away, in which Orlando had been hiding for the last five months.

He had known she would turn up at her aunt's home. It was the most logical place for her to go. So, he'd been waiting here for her to show up since two weeks after he had "died."

When she did, and he saw she was pregnant, he had been tempted to sneak into the house and rip Quinn's child from her belly. But that would've revealed his death was a lie. Too bad he'd had to eliminate Ortega. If the guy had still been around instead of buried in a grave outside Rio, Durrie probably would have sent him to do it.

Durrie leaned away from the telescope, wincing, and rubbed his forehead. Another one of his migraines was coming on. He walked into the kitchen and poured out four aspirin from the giant bottle he'd picked up, then downed them with a sip of whiskey.

Before Rio, the migraines had occurred once or twice a month at most, making it easy for him to hide them from Orlando. Afterward, he was getting them at least once a week, sometimes more.

Concerned, he'd taken a leave from observing his former girl-friend and spent a week in Singapore getting scanned and prodded and poked. In the end, he'd been given a clean bill of health. The doctor had said stress might be the cause and suggested taking a vacation.

Durrie decided not to worry so much about it. The migraines always went away soon enough.

He looked through the telescope again, then grinned.

"Hey, baby."

Orlando had just stepped outside, her brat strapped to her chest in one of those baby carriers. Her aunt was with them. It was Saturday morning, so per their normal schedule, they would be heading to the market.

Just another dull day in Orlandoville.

What he would give to have Quinn show up again. Durrie had feasted on the apparent falling out between the two on Orlando's porch a couple of weeks earlier. But Durrie knew his apprentice. If Quinn thought Orlando didn't want him here, he wouldn't return until she said it was okay.

A goddamn boy scout, but c'est la vie.

Durrie watched until Orlando, her aunt, and the brat disappeared from sight. He then walked over to the kitchen table, on which were stacks of maps and books and files and magazines. He took his usual seat and scanned the mounds of research.

Somewhere in here would be his way back to glory, and the means to deal with those who had wronged him.

It didn't matter that it would probably take years to implement whatever his plan turned out to be. His inevitable success was the only important thing.

He opened his journal, checked his notes, and picked up where he'd left off.